Belle Teal

Belle Teal

ANN M.
MARTIN

Scholastic Press — *New York*

Library of Congress Catalog Card Number 00–136292

ISBN 0-439 09823 8

10 9 8 7 6 5 4 3 2 1   01 02 03 04 05

Printed in the U.S.A.
First edition, October 2001

For my nephew,
Henry Raynsford McGrath, with love.

Special thanks to Liz Szabla, Jean Feiwel,
Laura Godwin, and especially to Pat Skarda,
who set the story in motion.

Belle Teal

One

Gran's vegetable garden has been a pure delight this year. I am sitting in the middle of it, and even though it is September, I am surrounded by bush beans and cucumbers and carrots and peppers and peas. We put the peas in early this year, Gran and me, so early that we had one good crop, and then we put in some more and had another good crop.

Gran, she is amazing, even if she has become a little forgetful. She can figure out how to do just about anything. And she can always see the good in people and situations, like in that song about accentuating the positive and eliminating the negative. Sometimes when our radio is not on, I hear Gran making her own music in our kitchen. She sings, "You got to ac-*cent*-tchu-ate the positive, e-*lim*-mi-nate the negative, and latch *on* to the affirmative. Don' mess with Mr. In Between . . ." Now me, I would sing at the top of my lungs, but Gran says that is not ladylike and she always sings nice and low and soft.

My journal is spread across my bare knees, but at this very moment I am not writing in it. My head is so stuffed full of birdsongs and insect music and thoughts about the last day of summer vacation that there is no room for concentrating on writing. Also, the sun is hot. Beating down hot. It has been one long, simmering summer. I don't remember a summer quite like it, here in our hills. Mama and Gran and me, we sleep most nights with the windows wide open, not caring about all the flies and mosquitoes and no-see-ums that fly inside to escape the heat with us.

I wiggle my toes in the dirt and inspect a scab on my knee. I wish Mama was home for my last day of summer freedom, but she went into Coker Creek this morning to begin her new job. Mama, she starts jobs like I start library books — one right after the other.

I think she is overlooking one of the key things about having a job, which is sticking with it. A library book is meant to be finished, but a job is meant to be stuck with. Mama means well, though. She just wants more for our family.

Our family has been Mama and Gran and me for as long as I can remember. Daddy, he died before I turned one, and Grandpop was gone before Mama married Daddy. But Mama and Gran and me make a very cozy family. And I like a family that is all women. Me and Gran are real close. We spend a lot of time together, since apart from switching jobs so frequently, Mama also usually works two to three jobs all at once, depending on the time of year. Waitressing, bartending, whatever she can find. This new job in Coker Creek, it's a maid's job, at that motel off Old Route 28, at the edge of town. If I know Mama, it won't satisfy her for long.

I pat my stomach. It is full from the lunch Gran just made. Also it is on the puffy side. I have increased in size over the summer. I wonder how I am going to fit into my first-day-of-school dress, which was also my last-day-of-school dress in June. Oh, well. I am not going to dwell on that. I am going to eliminate the negative. I believe I'll head on over to Clarice's house for the rest of the afternoon. I have done all my chores except for the evening ones, and anyway Gran, she has already said, "Belle Teal, you just enjoy today. Tomorrow your school responsibilities start again." Actually, she said that twice this morning, the second time with almost the exact same words she used the first time around, as if she didn't remember she had just said them half an hour before.

I ease back inside our little house and hide the journal under my mattress. Then I slip off my dirty shorts and pull on a pair of jeans. "Gran," I say as I poke my head in the kitchen, "I'm going to Clarice's."

Gran is mixing batter for corn bread. She is at the table, and the kitchen is so hot, I think I could suffocate in it. I can feel sweat forming under my hair and starting to slide down my forehead. But Gran stands there looking all tidy and cool-like. I hear her humming a tune I recognize as "G.I. Jive."

"Gran?" I say again. "I'm going to Clarice's."

Gran emerges from some kind of fog in her head. "Okay. Home by dinner . . . honey."

For just a second I have this spooky feeling that she might have forgotten my name. But I shoo the thought aside and run out our door, across our yard, and down to the dirt road. It's a two-mile walk to Clarice's, and I haven't bothered with shoes. By this time of summer the soles of my feet are so hard, I wouldn't need shoes for anything but warmth, and that is not an issue.

Clarice, she once told me she sometimes gets bored on the walk between our houses if she is alone. I can't imagine that. I always use the walk for thinking. Today I am thinking about tomorrow — about the first day of fifth grade at Coker Creek Elementary, the new colored students, and wonderful Miss Casey.

Clarice and me, we have been best friends since the beginning of kindergarten, which was way back in 1957. And we have been waiting since 1959 for Miss Casey to be our teacher. We have wished for her since the moment we set eyes on her, her first day at Coker Creek, when she arrived at school all dressed up and smelling of perfume that was probably from the country of France. None of the other teachers looked like Miss Casey. Or smelled like her. I fell in love with Miss Casey that day.

I walk along the dirt road, trying to avoid the bigger rocks, watching as grasshoppers zip ahead of me in the heated air. This is the easy part of the walk, going down our hill. Coming back from Clarice's will be another story. Tomorrow I will cover part of this trip on the school bus. I wonder if any of the new colored students will be on our bus route. I don't see how, but you never know.

It's funny. The only thing me and Clarice have been able to wrap our minds around this summer is the joyful thought of sitting in Miss Casey's class for a whole year. The only thing most other folks have wrapped their minds around is the notion of letting the Negro children into our school. So far those students have been going to the colored school over in Peapack, but starting this year, some of them will be coming to Coker Creek. It makes more sense. Coker Creek Elementary is much closer to those kids' homes than the school in Peapack is.

Mama says, "You be nice to those children, Belle Teal. They'll want to see smiling faces."

Why wouldn't I be nice to new students?

The road widens slightly toward the bottom of the hill. And when it meets up with Route 518, which if you turned left on it, would take you into the center of Coker Creek, it becomes a paved road. I cross 518 and soon I reach Clarice's father's auto body shop and then Miss Wanda's beauty salon, where sometimes I stop in for a grape soda and a chat with Miss Wanda. And then one, two, three houses, and there's Clarice's.

Clarice Baker meets me at the screen door before I even get to the top of the wooden steps. Those steps are painted a deep green, which I think is a lovely color, as lovely as the rest of Clarice's house. I wouldn't ever want to live anywhere except in our house in the hills with Mama and Gran, but there is something delicious about the Bakers' home. I step inside, into the dark coolness. Our house sits in a clearing and the sun beats down on it all day long. Clarice's house is surrounded by big shade trees, and in the summer the ceiling fans, one in almost every room, turn slowly, stirring the air.

Clarice and me, we step into the living room and the first thing I set my eyes on is the television. The Bakers got it almost three years ago. It is some invention. I have learned so much about life from what I have seen on it.

"Hey, Belle Teal," calls Clarice's sister from the kitchen.

"Hey, Shari," I reply. Shari is fifteen and will be a sophomore in high school.

"You ready for school tomorrow?" she asks. She is sitting at the table, putting pink nail polish on her fingers.

"Ready as I'll ever be," I reply.

"Do you girls want any help with your outfits?"

I glance at Clarice. "Well, no, I guess not. I think we're all set."

Now Shari, she is sweet to be so nice to Clarice and me. She always offers to help us with our looks, and I know she could do a good job because she is a real fashion plate herself. She is pretty and has a chest that she needs to contain with a bra, and boys call her on the phone all the time.

Me and Clarice never take her up on her offers of fashion help, but Shari doesn't seem to mind.

"Want a Coke?" Clarice asks me.

"Yes, thanks," I reply, all polite, since Shari is sitting there.

Clarice snags two bottles from the refrigerator and we take them back into the living room, where we sprawl on the floor.

"Is it time for *The Edge of Night?*" I ask.

"Not quite. I'll fill you in on the last few days."

Clarice watches *The Edge of Night* and *As the World Turns* as often as she can. I am not as interested in *As the World Turns,* but *The Edge of Night,* now that is really something. When Sarah Lane Karr died while saving her daughter, well, Clarice and me were breathless. We talked about it for days.

Four-thirty finally rolls around and the show starts. Shari rushes in from the kitchen, waving her fingers in the air so's to dry her nails, and Mrs. Baker hurries inside from the back garden, where she has been weeding in her straw hat. We all sit absolutely silently for one half hour, until five o'clock when the show ends and we can breathe again. Clarice and me have been grasping hands, and now we let go and wipe off the sweat on our jeans. Those Karrs are quite a family.

Shari switches off the television and a few minutes later Mr. Baker steps through the front door, kind of grimy from his day at the auto shop.

"Hello, Bakers!" he greets us, and he means me as well as the others. He says he considers me an honorary Baker and his third daughter.

"Hello!" we all reply.

"Mama, can Belle Teal stay for dinner?" asks Clarice, even though she knows she isn't supposed to ask right in front of me in case her mother doesn't want a guest for some reason.

Before Mrs. Baker can answer, though, I say, "Thanks, but I better get on home. I don't want Gran to have to eat alone."

"Where's your mama at?" Shari wants to know.

"New job," I tell her.

Nobody asks any questions. They are used to Mama.

I stand up. "Thank you for the Coke," I say. "See you in the morning, Clarice."

"I'll save you a seat on the bus," she replies.

"You all are going to have some day tomorrow," says Shari thoughtfully. "I wonder if any of those Negro children will be on your bus."

Mr. Baker sits down on the couch next to Mrs. Baker. "Doesn't matter whether they're Negro children or not, Shari," he says. "They're all just children."

Mr. Baker says this so gentle that it doesn't sound like a scolding.

I scoot out the door then and begin the walk back home.

Two

I am not expecting to see Mama until my bedtime that night. When she left for her new job this morning she said her very first day of work at the R U Sleep Inn was going to be a double shift. But when I come trudging across our yard after that walk home from Clarice's there is our car parked off to the side of the house.

Suddenly my tiredness slides away and I pick up speed and run on inside. "Mama!" I cry.

She's sitting at the kitchen table smoking one of her Salem cigarettes, dropping ashes into a grape jelly jar that we use as a drinking glass, and so Gran is sneaking little frowns at her. And she's wearing this turquoise uniform that has ADELE stitched across a pocket on the front. Now isn't that something. Strangers who have never met Mama before are introduced to her as Adele. That is not right. They should be introduced to her as Mrs. Harper. Immediately I tell my mind not to see Mama in that uniform, but instead in her red polka-dotted dress, the one she wears with the beautiful wide shiny patent-leather belt.

"Hi, precious," Mama greets me. She leans down to brush her lips across my hair and I smell cigarette smoke and something else. Maybe Lysol.

"Hi, Mama," I say. "I thought you had to work a double shift."

Mama shakes her head. "Mr. Titus got a notion. Changed everyone's schedules today."

I am not sure what to say. I'm glad Mama's here for dinner. But we could have used that double-shift money.

Gran eyes the cigarette and says, "Adele, honey, put that thing out now or go outside with it. The kitchen smells like a chimney."

"You need help with supper, Gran?" I ask, hoping she'll say no. I look around and see that while I was at

Clarice's, Gran has gone to the vegetable garden and picked lettuce and tomatoes for salad, and has shelled a bowlful of peas. The corn bread is just about ready, and one of our chickens is roasting in the oven.

"No, thanks, honey," Gran replies. And she adds, "Adele, we are almost out of sugar. Can you pick some up tomorrow?"

Mama rises from the table, taking her cigarette and the jelly glass with her. "Sure, Mama Belle," she says. And I feel that little prick of pride I feel every time I am reminded that I was named for my gran. She is Belle Teal Rodes, and I am Belle Teal Harper.

Mama and me, we settle in on the old porch swing. Mama swings and puffs out smoke, and I swing and think about what Mr. Baker said as I was leaving Clarice's.

"Mama?"

"Yeah, precious?" Mama sucks on her cigarette. Her nails are painted red, and they would match her patent-leather belt if she was wearing it. Mama cares about fashion in the way Shari does.

"Today at Clarice's," I begin, "Shari, she wondered will any Negro children be on our bus tomorrow, and Mr. Baker, *he* said don't think of them as Negro children because they're all just children."

"Huh," says Mama. "Good for Mr. Baker." She stares off into the hills and blows out a stream of smoke.

"Mama, how many Neg — I mean, how many new kids will be at our school tomorrow?"

"Three," replies Mama.

"Any of them in my class?"

"I'm not sure, precious."

"Mama, why did you tell me to be nice to the new children? You said, 'They'll want to see smiling faces.' I wouldn't be mean to a new kid. Least, not unless the new kid was mean first."

Mama drags on her cigarette. "Huh," she says again. "You are absolutely right." She starts to say something else, then stops, lets out a sigh.

Gran appears at the screen door behind us and says, "Adele, honey, can you stop and pick us up some sugar tomorrow? We are almost out."

"Gran!" I exclaim. "You —" But Mama, she lays her hand on mine quick-like, so I don't say anything more.

Gran disappears into the kitchen.

"About the new children, Belle Teal," says Mama. "You just keep in mind that our family does not judge people by their appearances. We don't want to be judged that way, and we don't judge others that way."

"Yes, ma'am."

I want to ask about a million more questions, but Mama has gotten that far-off look in her eyes. Conversations with Mama only last so long.

I think that now the front porch is smelling like a chimney too, so I go on back into the kitchen. Gran is standing by the table, gazing out the window, up our hill.

"What is it, Gran?" I ask, thinking she sees an animal. Maybe a coyote.

Slowly her focus shifts back to me. "Oh," is all she says.

"Is dinner ready?"

"Yes, indeed. Go get your mother. But tell her she can't come to the table unless she's clean," which is Gran's way of saying Mama had better put that cigarette out.

A few minutes later, Mama and Gran and me are sitting around the table, holding hands. Gran's eyes are squeezed tight shut as she says, "Heavenly Father, bless this food to our use and us to Thy service. We beg for Christ's sake. Amen." I am watching Gran, who looks so holy when she is conversing with the Lord. Mama is gazing out the window. She probably has Mr. Titus and double shifts and other work things on her mind.

When the blessing is over we dig into the food. I don't know how Gran manages to put together our meals day in and day out. Mama, she earns the money for what food we have to buy, but Gran, she is in charge of the cooking, and as far as I can see that is some job. I reach across the table and give Gran's hand a pat.

"Now, what is that for, Belle Teal?" she asks me with a little smile.

"Nothing," I say, with a smile back.

Mama looks up and smiles at both of us. Then she says to me, "All ready for school?"

"Yes, ma'am."

"You got enough pencils and things?"

"I think so."

"And you finally have Miss Casey."

"Yes!"

"Who all is going to be in your class this year?" Gran wants to know.

"Oh, you know. All the regulars," I say. "Clarice. And Little Boss. And Chas and Vernon." I make a face.

"Belle Teal . . ." says Mama with a warning in her voice.

"I am not judging Chas and Vernon based on their appearance," I tell her. "I am judging them based on what's inside. I know their insides and they're mean." I think for a moment. "Mama, is it wrong to hate someone —" I start to ask.

"It is wrong to hate anyone," Mama replies quickly.

"But is it wrong to hate someone because that person hates other people?"

Mama sighs. She looks like she wishes she had a cigarette. "Hate just creates more hate," she says finally.

I think of those school meetings Mama went to over the summer. The meetings the parents held after it was announced that the colored students would be going to Coker Creek in the fall. Mama couldn't get to all the meetings, but she got to some of them. And she came home from them looking tired and a little angry. She said she didn't think she was a very popular person. But when Mama believes something she sticks to her guns about it. And she speaks up. Says the Lord gave her a mouth and she intends to put it to good use.

"Sounds like everyone is putting their mouths to

good use," I told her after one meeting. "Only most people have something different to say than you do."

"I know." Mama didn't talk too much about those meetings.

And eventually it didn't seem to matter who thought what, because it turned out the colored students were going to go to Coker Creek in any case. "It's not the parents' decision to make," said Mama. "It's the law. Although I'm sure the parents will have more to say on the subject."

Now Gran puts down her fork and directs her gaze at Mama. "You don't think there'll be any trouble at school tomorrow, do you?" she asks.

Mama shakes her head. "Nope. It's all died down. Besides, this isn't Little Rock."

"Little Rock? The Little Rock Nine?" I say. Everyone has heard about the Little Rock Nine, the nine colored students who were chosen to integrate Central High School in Little Rock, Arkansas, a few years back.

"Those poor children," murmurs Gran. "Heavens. What they went through. . . . Oh! Adele, honey, I just remembered. We are almost out of sugar. Tomorrow could you stop and pick us up another bag?"

I look at Mama with my mouth hanging open, but I know enough not to say anything. I can't bear to hear Mama patiently answer Gran, though, so I scoot my plate over to the sink, grab my journal, and head for the front porch.

"Belle Teal!" Mama calls after me. "The dishes."

"Can I write first, please? Before the sun goes down?"

"Yeah, precious. Okay." Mama only sounds a little exasperated.

On our porch I sit in the old lawn chair, the one with the scratchy green and white strips that are coming apart. I draw my legs up underneath me and open my journal in my lap. I don't lift my pen right away, though. I take in a deep breath and look out over our hills. I think how Gran has lived in these hills all her whole life. She can tell you everything about them — their weather and their trees and their animals. Gran, she reads the weather with one finger and her nose. Every morning she stands on the porch, holds up one thin pointer finger, and sniffs the air. "Hot today," she'll say. Or, "Snow coming." Or, "No rain yet." Lately, though, her predictions haven't made much sense. For instance, this morning she stood here in the little light summer nightie that is the only one she'll wear anymore, put her finger in the air, sniffed, and then looked at our broken thermometer, the one that's been stuck on forty degrees for three years now. And she said, "My land, only forty. It's going to be downright chilly today."

Now Gran knows as well as Mama and me that that thermometer is broken, so I don't know what's got into her head. It's a good thing I pick up on facts pretty easy, because these days I have to sort out the facts from Gran's new brand of fiction.

I pick up my pen. I start to write about how I don't look a thing like Gran. Gran is all skinny and birdish. Tiny too. And before her hair went white it was pure blonde. I've seen pictures of her as a girl. Me, I'm darker, like Mama, and I'm a bit on the plump side, which I guess I take after my daddy. Plus, I'm growing fast as a weed right now. Soon I'll be taller than Gran.

I am writing all this when behind me I hear Gran ask Mama about that sugar again and I want to leap up out of the chair and shake Gran by her bony shoulders. Then I think to myself about what Mama has said to me so many times: "We have faced lots of hardships, Belle Teal. You and your gran and I. But we can take care of ourselves. We do whatever is necessary. We have strength and patience."

I look up at the sky. I don't know if there is a God up there or not. Gran is sure her Lord resides there, but I am still making up my mind. I know I get some comfort from looking at the sky, though. So I gaze at the streaky clouds turning salmon pink as the sun drops low, and I tell myself to have strength and patience where Gran is concerned. While I am at it, I wish that a little strength and patience would flow into the minds of the people who are making judgments about the colored students, and then I wish for extra strength and patience for the colored students themselves.

I write a few more sentences in my journal. Then I go inside to do my chores and get ready for my first day of fifth grade.

Three

The sun wakes me the next morning. I jump out of
bed in a big hurry. It is going to be another blazing hot
day, and I imagine sticky seats and desktops, and
heavy air hanging in our classroom. But mostly I think
about Miss Casey and how wonderful fifth grade is going to be. I pull on my green shift, the one Gran made
for me in the spring. It wasn't the best-looking shift
then, and five months later I am starting to pop out
of it in a few places. I jam my feet into my old brown
boots. They are the only shoes I ever wear, no matter
what the season, when I bother with shoes at all.

"Precious, why don't you let me braid your hair?" is Mama's greeting to me as I sit down to Gran's breakfast of eggs and biscuits.

"Oh, Mama," I say. Braiding always takes so long.

"Just for your first day of school," she says.

I think of standing there while Mama tugs and pulls. "I look okay," I tell her finally, and Mama gives up.

I suspect I am not looking my best for the first day of school. I don't think Miss Casey will mind loose hair, though.

When breakfast is over (I always eat a good, big breakfast), I rush around gathering up the things I will need for school: notebook, pencil case, change-purse, lunch in a bag.

"Bye, Mama! Bye, Gran!" I call as I run out the door. I fly across our yard and wait by the road. I can see the school bus wheezing up our hill.

The bus draws to a stop and I wave madly at Bernette, the driver, before she even opens the door.

"Hello, Bernette!" I cry as I board those three steps.

"Welcome back, Belle Teal," she says, and she flashes me a wide grin.

Bernette and me, we never get to see each other over the summer.

I give Bernette a peck on the cheek and then I stand at the head of the aisle and look at the faces in the bus, trying to spot Clarice. Just as I see her waving to me from the third row of seats I hear something like a little snort down at my side. Sitting in the very first row of seats, directly behind Bernette, is a girl I have never seen before.

Lordy, she is proper looking.

I glance at my shift with the stitches popping apart and the stain on the hem, and at my dusty boots. Then I look at the new girl again. Her blonde hair is silky and shiny and pulled back from her face with a yellow-and-white-striped ribbon. And she is wearing an outfit I think I might have seen in the Sears catalog — a yellow skirt-and-sweater set, very soft looking. And black shoes that are patent leather like Mama's belt. And white tights. By lunchtime this girl is going to be roasting.

I can't help myself. I stare at her. I look at her hair ribbon, and then my eyes glide all the way down to those shoes, then back up to the ribbon.

The girl looks me in the eye and snorts again. Snorts like a pig.

I frown at her.

"Nice dress," she whispers as I start to pass by her.

"Who are you?" I ask.

"I am Vanessa Mathers, and I come from Mechanicsville."

"Nice to meet you," I reply. I head for Clarice.

While this has been going on, Bernette has been engaged in the daily struggle that takes place in front of my house. She has to turn the bus around. I am the only kid who lives up here on the hill, so after Bernette reaches my stop, she groans and pants and lets out sighs that puff up her gray bangs while drips of sweat form on her temples. She turns and turns and turns that steering wheel as she swings the bus into our drive, backs it up, and heads us down the hill again.

I am fully settled next to Clarice before Vanessa Mathers realizes what Bernette has been up to. Vanessa turns around and glares at me. "You mean we had to drive all the way up here just to pick *you* up?" she asks.

I think about my conversations with Mama the night before — about being nice to new kids and hate creating hate and all. I don't want to judge Vanessa on her appearance, but I believe she is judging me on mine. Which I don't like it. Chas and Vernon, for instance, they got to know me before they showed their mean selves. Still, I decide to hold my tongue for the present. I just smile sweet like at Vanessa Mathers.

Vanessa, she makes quite a face at me before she swings her shiny hair around and rides the rest of the way to Coker Creek Elementary with her eyes fixed on the back of Bernette's head.

Clarice and me shrug our shoulders at each other. Then we start gabbing away. Mostly about Miss Casey, but also we try to figure out what will happen on *The Edge of Night* this afternoon. We manage to ignore Chas and Vernon, who are sitting in the very last row of seats throwing spitballs down the bus aisle. One hits Vanessa Mathers and I know she feels it, because she squirms her head just a little, but she will not turn around and look. Only when Bernette glances at the boys in the enormous rearview mirror and says quietly, "Enough," do the boys finally stop. That Bernette, she could be a principal or something.

By the time Bernette pulls up in front of Coker Creek Elementary, Clarice and me are busting with excitement.

"Let's try to sit in the first row," I say. "Next to each other. And right in front of Miss Casey."

"Okay."

We wave good-bye to Bernette and skitter off the bus.

Then we come to a screeching halt.

Parents — I guess they are parents — are lined up along the walkway to the front doors of Coker Creek. Me and Clarice will have to pass between them, like we are in a parade.

Clarice frowns at me. She pushes her blue glasses nervously up and down the bridge of her nose. "What's going on?" she asks.

"Don't know."

The parents are standing there, watching the kids that stream off the buses or climb out of cars. They are not saying a word, but their faces are thunder-clouds. A few of them have handmade signs, which they are not holding up yet. I try to read them upside down. I think I see a lot of words that begin with N, but I am afraid to stare at the signs for too long.

I feel my face grow warm, like I'm embarrassed, even though I haven't done anything. And I know the underarms of my shift are turning a darker shade of green because now I'm sweating. I jam my hands down at my sides so no one will see.

"Come on," I say to Clarice, and we walk fast inside the building, and directly to room 6

The door to our classroom is open, and someone has hung a huge yellow paper sun on it. Written on the sun is:

Room 6, Grade 5
Miss Casey
WELCOME!

All those questions that were forming on my tongue — the ones about the angry parents and their signs — melt away at the sight of Miss Casey at her desk. Clarice and me, we zoom into the room and slide into two seats next to each other, right in front of Miss Casey. We can barely see her, though. A bunch of kids are clustered around her and she's talking quietly to them, smiling.

"Hey." A soft voice behind me. A nudge on my shoulder.

I turn around. There is Little Boss. "Hey!" I cry.

Me and Little Boss have not seen each other all summer. (There's a lot of people I don't see all summer.) I grin at him. We have been friends since he moved here just after third grade began. Not everyone likes Little Boss, but I do. Despite his faults, which are many. Whenever those faults come rearing up, I remind myself about what goes on at Little Boss's house. Now, I have never actually been at his house, but in a town the size of Coker Creek, everybody pretty much knows everybody else's business, or thinks they do, and a lot of what a person hears is true. Chas, he used to live next door to Little Boss. This was before Chas's father started his painting business and made enough money to buy a house closer on in to town. Chas and Little Boss got to be friends, and Chas, he used to tell me and Clarice what he would hear on the nights Big Boss had been out drinking. I do not know how Little Boss lives with so much anger in his house, except that he doesn't have any choice.

Clarice, she thinks it's kind of strange that Little Boss and me wound up friends, and to tell the truth, I'm not even sure how that happened. All I know is that by the end of third grade, just about the time Chas's family moved, me and Little Boss were talking on the playground almost every day. One thing about me is I am a good listener. That's what Clarice says. Little Boss, he doesn't usually tell me anything profound. Maybe it's just that he knows he could if he ever wanted to.

"How was your summer?" Little Boss asks me now.

"Good. Yours?"

"Good." He grins at me.

I am about to ask Little Boss what he did over the summer, knowing he'll answer me with, "Nothing," when there is a scuffle around Miss Casey's desk. She is standing up and the kids who have been talking to her drift away to find seats. I sit down in my chair fast, proud of myself for having claimed a desk in this prime location. Then I give a wave to Little Boss as he heads for the back of the room with Chas and Vernon. I bet they won't get away with sitting together there for long.

Miss Casey is straightening things on her desk. As I watch her, I feel like when I am in our yard and I see a rabbit or a toad or something and it doesn't see me, and I have a chance to observe it up close. Miss Casey, she is wearing the most wonderful rose-colored dress with a string of pearls around her neck. She has tiny gold bands on two of her fingers (*not* on her wedding band finger, though), and from back here at my desk I can smell a very light scent, which it must be her perfume from France.

I wonder all sorts of things about Miss Casey — where she lives, where she is from, who her friends are, what she eats for dinner, where she goes shopping. I have a tiny daydream about her in which she turns out to be my long-lost aunt.

I do love Miss Casey.

Suddenly I hear a low roar from outside, voices raised, and I turn to look out the window. Miss Casey stops fiddling around at her desk and looks out the window too. Over to the left I can see some of those parents. Now they remind me of a swarm of bees whose hive has been disturbed. I watch Miss Casey watching them until I realize that someone is sitting down at the desk next to me, not the desk Clarice has taken, but the one on my right. I turn my head.

Looking back at me is Vanessa Mathers.

"Oh." I groan.

Vanessa gives me a large fake smile, smoothes her skirt across her lap, places her notebook neatly in her desk, then folds her hands in front of her.

I turn to Clarice and tug at her sleeve. "Guess who's in our class," I whisper.

But Clarice is not looking at me. She's not looking outside either. Her eyes are glued to the doorway to our room.

"Clarice," I whisper urgently.

Clarice glances at me, raises her eyebrows, and looks back at the door, so finally I follow her gaze.

Standing uncertainly in front of that yellow sun is a colored boy. Right behind him, with her hands placed gently on his shoulders, is a colored lady. "Excuse me," she says, quiet-like. "Are you Miss Casey?"

Miss Casey turns away from the window. When she sees the lady and the boy, a wide smile spreads across her face.

"Mrs. Craig?" she says. "Darryl? Welcome. Welcome to our class."

Four

"Darryl, say good morning to your teacher." Mrs. Craig nudges him toward Miss Casey.

Darryl sticks out his hand. "Good morning, ma'am," he says, solemn-like. "Pleased to meet you."

"Pleased to meet *you*," replies Miss Casey. She turns on that beautiful smile again as she bends over to shake his hand. Then she leaves Darryl standing at the front of our classroom as she leads Mrs. Craig toward the door. The grown-ups talk for a couple of minutes, but I can't hear what they're saying. Mrs. Craig, she looks dead scared, though, and I don't blame her a bit. But Miss Casey places her hand on Mrs. Craig's arm while she talks to her, and soon I see Mrs. Craig's eyes soften.

Meanwhile, Darryl, he just stands there, staring down at his feet.

From the back row I hear whispering and snickering. And Vanessa turns a look on Darryl that is so hateful, I can almost feel poison shooting out of her eyes. I flash her a mean glare of my own, and what does she do but look straight at me and smile another one of her fake smiles.

Miss Casey turns around. The snickering stops.

Mrs. Craig says, "I'll be back at the end of the day, Darryl," and she walks out of our room, her back straight, her head high.

Miss Casey shows Darryl to the only empty desk in the room. I don't know how she manages it, but as she is pulling out his chair for him, she also turns and sweeps her eyes around the room, glancing at every single one of us, sending out a warning about snickering and poison-eye looks.

Now, Little Boss, he is in rare bad form, because what does he do as soon as Miss Casey's back is toward him, but make a great show of hauling his desk away from Darryl's. He pushes it so hard, he nearly bangs into the back of poor Stephen Haines, who will cry at the drop of a hat but, fortunately, this time does nothing. Chas, who's on the other side of Little Boss's desk, starts brushing off his sleeves, like Darryl has somehow wafted cooties on Chas's shirt just by moving the air in the room. Vernon, meanwhile, has been working away at a drawing of a person with black skin and enormous lips. He holds it up for us to see, but by now Miss Casey has reached her desk again, and as she turns to face us, Vernon shoves the picture under his notebook.

"Good morning, class," says Miss Casey brightly. "Now that we're all here, I want to greet you officially. Ray Stomper, please move your desk to its original position.

"Welcome to fifth grade," Miss Casey continues cheerfully, not even watching Little Boss as he edges his desk reluctantly back toward Darryl's. "I think we are going to have an exciting year."

That Miss Casey, she doesn't miss a trick. She probably knows about Vernon's picture too. I gaze at her, at her pearls and her dress and her perfect chestnut-colored hair, and just drink in the sight of her as she leads us in the Pledge of Allegiance to the flag and takes our milk orders. As she is walking around the room a few minutes later, telling us what all we're going to be learning this year, she lifts up Vernon's notebook, removes the picture, and carries it to her desk, where she leaves it wrong side up on top of a pile of papers. I myself would have been both humiliated and dumbfounded, but Vernon, he turns to Chas and just shakes his head in disgust.

After Miss Casey finishes telling us about the American history and fractions and tall tales and mammals we'll be learning about, she says, "Now, class, I am going to assign permanent seats to you."

I hear a few quiet groans, and Vanessa Mathers puts her hand primly in the air. "Ma'am, what if somebody likes the seat she has already chosen?" she asks.

"I hope she will like the new seat just as well," replies Miss Casey. "I have studied this and given it a lot of thought and decided that the new seating arrangement will be for the best."

I realize that Miss Casey has been busy over the summer. One thing, she must have learned a lot about her students. Otherwise, how would she know who Little Boss is? Then I realize that Miss Casey didn't even need to take attendance. I feel a thrill when I think that Miss Casey has been studying up on me in her free time.

Miss Casey, she starts walking around the room. As she passes each desk, she taps it, and says the name of the person she wants to sit at it. When she is finished, Clarice is in the row behind me, which is a shame, but Vanessa is clear on the other side of the room, so that's good. And I am kind of in the front — in the second row — but not opposite Miss Casey's desk anymore. I really wanted to continue to observe her up close. And to be able to look at all the things on her desk — to see if she has a rubber-band ball, to see what condition her eraser is in (probably not chewed on like mine), or if maybe she has any interesting trinkets.

Little Boss, Chas, and Vernon have been separated, and now only Chas is in the back row. Miss Casey has placed Darryl in the seat where Clarice just was, right up against the front of her desk. He's in between Vanessa, whose desk is on the end by the windows, and Mae Bender, who's in the seat I wanted. A full row separates him from Little Boss and Vernon, and two rows separate him from Chas. I decide Miss

Casey has been studying us very hard and is smart in addition to being beautiful and smelling good.

Now I am watching Vanessa, who has slid her chair as far away from Darryl as possible (I guess she knows better than to move her desk, like Little Boss did), and again I'm remembering Mama saying to be nice to the colored children. That Vanessa, she certainly is one for judging. I'm beginning to think her insides aren't so different from Chas's and Vernon's insides, even though their outsides are mighty different. Mama's words make more and more sense.

"Girls and boys," says Miss Casey, breaking into my thoughts, "we have two new students in our class this year. Their names are Vanessa Mathers and Darryl Craig. I want you to make them feel at home. And Vanessa and Darryl, I'd like you to come up here and tell us a few things about yourselves. Who will go first?"

Vanessa shoots her arm in the air and wiggles her fingers around.

Miss Casey looks at Darryl, but he is sitting with his hands folded on top of his desk, staring at the blackboard. "Very well. Vanessa . . ." she says, pointing to a spot under the American flag.

Vanessa slides out of her seat like a graceful swan

and stands before us. Miss Casey stands next to her and puts her arm around her, which makes me jealous. *"Bonjour, mes amis,"* begins Vanessa, looking out at our class. "In case you don't know, that's French. French for 'Hello, my friends.'"

"Who does she think she is? The queen?" whispers Junie Partridge, who is sitting next to me.

Vanessa waves one hand in the air, queen-like, and says, "I hail from Mechanicsville. I lived my entire life there. I have a younger brother named . . ."

"Prince Heraldium," Junie supplies in a whisper only I can hear.

". . . Joseph Crew Mathers, and my full name is Vanessa Amy Wynona Mathers. I am named for my beautiful mama. My daddy manages the grain company in Mechanicsville. It is a very important job. We hope to be happy here in the little town of Coker Creek. I am sure I am going to enjoy being a student at Coker Creek Elementary. *Merci beaucoup.* And *s'il vous plaît,* feel free to sit with me for *dejeuner* this afternoon."

"Thank you, Vanessa," says Miss Casey. She looks out at the rest of us and I suddenly feel small and plain. "Does anyone have any questions for Vanessa?"

I imagine that I have eyes in the back of my head and they are looking at Clarice in the row behind me, sending her a message about stuck-up French-speaking goody-goodies with fancy names and airs. I don't turn around, though. I am determined to get off on the right foot in fifth grade. But how I wish I could speak French in order to impress Miss Casey.

I can't tell, though, if Miss Casey is impressed with the French words. She is simply waiting for somebody to ask a question.

Mae Bender's arm flies up. "Where did you learn to speak French? Have you been to France?"

"To Paris."

Well.

"Twice," adds Vanessa.

My land.

I think that she really does sound like the queen. Queen Vanessa. Her Royal Highness. HRH Vanessa Mathers.

Next, puny little Stephen Haines puts his hand up. "Where else you traveled?" He asks this almost in a whisper.

"Oh, to London and Rome. All over Europe, really."

Mae's hand is in the air again. "Will you sit with me and Kayla at lunch today?" she asks, all eager.

"Why, certainly. I would be delighted to join you," replies HRH.

Mae sends a big satisfied grin over to Kayla, who's sitting in front of me.

This time I cannot help myself. I swivel around and peer at Clarice. I believe my mouth is actually hanging open with my disbelief. Clarice, she is looking back at me and her forehead is arranged in a frown. I don't want Miss Casey to catch us, though, so I fix my attention on HRH like she's a fascinating worm under a magnifying glass.

"Thank you," says Miss Casey when the questions have died down. "That was very interesting." She indicates that Vanessa should take her seat. Then she looks at Darryl. "Are you ready?" she asks him gently, and she points to that spot under the flag.

Vanessa, she is still on her way back to her seat, and when Darryl stands up, she leaps aside to escape him. Miss Casey sees this, but she doesn't comment on it. She just waits until Darryl is standing beside her, then puts her arm around his shoulders like she did Vanessa's, and smiles at him.

"Um, well," begins Darryl in a soft voice, "my name is Darryl Isaac Craig, and I live with my mother and my father. My father is a machinist and he works nights, and my mother works at the hospital in Mechanicsville. My aunt and uncle live next door to us." Darryl looks up at Miss Casey. She nods. "Well, I — I'm ten years old and I used to go to school in Peapack." He pauses. "That's all."

Our classroom is absolutely silent. I don't know which is worse. That awful snickering from before, or this silence that is so big and heavy, you could pick it up and throw it around the room.

Miss Casey, she gives us a prompt. "Does anyone have a question for Darryl?"

The silence grows.

Actually, I have several questions for Darryl. I want to know what is a machinist, and I wonder is he really another only child like me, and is the hospital his mother works at Baptist Memorial, because that is where I had my appendix out three years ago and maybe I met her then. But no hands are shooting into the air, so I leave mine resting in my desk, fiddling with an old crayon I have just found in the back.

Miss Casey is looking uncomfortable herself, or maybe a little mad. Finally she says, "Darryl, I have a question for you. What do you like to do in your spare time?"

"Ma'am, I like drawing, mostly."

"Drawing! Wonderful! Perhaps you will become our class artist."

Our room is as still as midnight. After looking out at our silent faces, Miss Casey, she finally says, "Class, I hope you will make Darryl feel welcome." Which I notice she did not feel the necessity of saying after Vanessa finished talking. Miss Casey gazes long and hard at us, but her eyes linger on Little Boss, Chas, and Vernon.

Five

Lordy, I do wish for my journal. So much is happening today that I can't keep apace of it all. I brought the journal to school once last year, but Vernon got ahold of it and read a choice selection aloud on the playground. Since then, the journal has never left our house and I just have to try to hang on to thoughts with my brain until I can grab a quiet moment somewheres at home.

All morning long I keep one eye on Miss Casey and whatever she is doing. I keep the other eye on Darryl, the kids in our class, and, outside the window, a small group of parents who are walking around and around. Now they are holding up those signs and chanting. It is a while before I get a good glimpse of one of the signs, since I don't want Miss Casey to catch me looking out the window.

The sign says, Niggers Go Home.

When I read that, I feel something in my stomach, like a punch.

I look over at Darryl. His eyes are fixed on Miss Casey, who is about to pass out our Think and Do books.

HRH Vanessa raises her hand. "Miss Casey," she says, "it is so awfully hot in here. I am about to expire. Could we please open a window?"

That is when I notice that, even though it is another hot-as-blazes day, every window in our classroom is shut. Miss Casey, she glances toward the parents outside. Then she puts on a bright smile and says, "Well, I can do better than that." And she hauls a big fan to the front of the room and turns it on. A few papers riffle up and go flying, but that breeze, it feels like a drink of Gran's lemonade. Plus, the hum of the fan drowns out the sound of the chanting. Then Miss Casey, looking even brighter, says, "I have another idea. Let's pull the shades down to keep out the sunlight."

She does that and I don't know if the room cools down any, but of course now the parents have been completely shut out of our view. I relax myself a little. Darryl looks like he relaxes too. His shoulders loosen up and he finally unclasps his hands.

I turn my full attention to Miss Casey and leave it there until she says, "Girls and boys, it is time for lunch. Please line up to go to the cafeteria."

The Coker Creek cafeteria is big enough to hold three classes at once. When all of us fourth-, fifth-, and sixth-graders pile on in there, that room is a madhouse. Even with cafeteria monitors poking around. You can either bring your lunch, or you can buy the hot lunch. Also, you can buy milk or ice cream. The hot lunch costs twenty-five cents and ice cream costs a nickel. You can imagine that I don't get to buy those things too often. Milk only costs two cents, though, so most days I go off to school with milk money. Gran, she sets two pennies by my place at the breakfast table, and I drop them in the changepurse I wear on a chain around my neck and keep tucked under my dress. About once a month I find a quarter by my place, and I put it in the purse and wait for the next time pizza burgers are being served.

Today I just have milk money. But Gran, she has packed me up a tasty lunch.

"You buying lunch?" I ask Clarice as we enter the cafeteria.

Clarice holds out her empty hands to remind me that she did not bring a lunch.

"Okay. I'll save us a table," I tell her.

We sit with Junie Partridge, and Mary Lee Hickerson, who's in sixth grade.

After we've got our straws unwrapped and all, the first thing Mary Lee asks us is, "You got any of the niggers in your class?"

I raise my eyebrows at Clarice.

Junie, she answers, "Yup. One. We also got us a princess."

Mary Lee doesn't take the bait. She couldn't care less about a princess. "Where is it?" she asks. *It.* She means Darryl. "One of the others is in my sister's class. When Mama finds out, she's going to throw a fit. She said she'd pull us out of school if we had to sit with one of them."

I am so mad that at first I can't think of a thing to say. But words don't fail me for long. I stand up. "And *my* mama," I say, "said she would pull me out of school if I had to sit with someone like you. Since I don't want to leave Coker Creek, I better go eat at a different table."

I move to one nearby. Clarice follows me, of course. Behind us, I can hear Mary Lee saying to Junie, "What does she mean, someone like me?" She doesn't get it at all.

I look around the cafeteria for Darryl. Finally I spot him at a table in the corner. He's sitting with two other colored kids, a boy and a girl, Miss Casey, and Mrs. Geary, who teaches fourth grade. I notice that there are a lot of empty tables around them.

Clarice and me finish our lunches quickly and run out to the playground behind the school.

"Want to play Four Square?" asks Clarice.

I do, but I am nervous because I can hear those parents chanting on the other side of the school. I am afraid they will try to come through to the playground, even though I don't really think anyone will let them in the building. Then I spot Darryl. He and the two other kids are being shown onto the playground by Mrs. Geary. I see Little Boss, Chas, and Vernon nearby.

Uh-oh, I think. But Mrs. Geary stands by the colored kids. Doesn't leave them for a minute.

Little Boss, Chas, and Vernon won't take their eyes off the kids.

By the time recess is over and we are back in our classroom, I feel wrung out. I am glad for our fan and our pulled-down shades. Glad that Little Boss, Chas, and Vernon are sitting where they can't touch Darryl. I sigh, even though Gran says sighing is unnecessary and tiresome.

And then Miss Casey does a grand thing. She gives us an assignment. Most of the kids in the room groan. But I gaze at Miss Casey in wonderment. She assigns us to write our autobiographies that night.

"Just two pages to tell me about yourselves and your lives. I want to get to know you better. I am going to write my autobiography too. I will share it with you tomorrow."

Well, I am dying. Because now I am going to find out all about Miss Casey. Where she grew up and who was in her family and like that. It is a dream come true. Plus, I will have fun writing my own auto-biography.

When the last bell of the day rings, my heart gives a jump. I don't want to go outside where those parents are circling around. Clarice, she must be feeling nervous too, because she loops her arm through mine and we walk out of our classroom side by side. I sneak one last look over my shoulder at Miss Casey, who is working at her desk, and I call to her, shy-like, "Bye!"

"Good-bye, girls. I'll see you tomorrow," she replies.

"Come on," says Clarice. "Let's hurry."

We will run by those parents fast, like they are the graveyard on Route 518.

I am surprised when we hustle through the front doors and I see the crowd outside. It is not as big as it had seemed before. Really, there are only about twelve or thirteen people. Most of them are women. But a couple of them are men who probably work the night shift. Or maybe they are out of work altogether.

The crowd is sort of muttering and murmuring, but that's all. I feel more confident. I un-loop my arm from Clarice's and we head toward our bus.

That's when I notice the old brown pickup truck and the man sitting in the driver's seat. I grab Clarice again. "Big Boss," I whisper.

We stop dead in our tracks, so that HRH Vanessa runs into us from behind. She snorts at me and goes on her way.

I stare at the truck and Little Boss's father.

"What's he doing here?" I say.

"Must have come to pick up Little Boss," Clarice answers.

"Means he's out of work again." Which is not a good thing for Little Boss. It's just him and his daddy, and Little Boss tries to steer clear of Big Boss. When Big Boss isn't working, that's much harder.

Big Boss waves one arm out the window of the truck. "Hey!" he calls, and I realize Little Boss is a few yards in front of Clarice and me.

Little Boss slows down, stiffens just a bit. He puts his hand in the air, though, and waves to Big Boss.

Big Boss, he doesn't see. His eyes have shifted slightly, caught sight of something, and narrowed. "You! You, boy!" he shouts. "You go back to where you belong."

I see Darryl then. Darryl and the two other colored kids. And the three grown ups who have arrived to walk them home.

"Your kind don't belong here!" calls one of the parents from the crowd. She's holding a bent sign in one fist, and shaking the other.

And then, Big Boss, he opens the door of his truck, jumps down, and spits on Darryl. Darryl looks up, wide-eyed, at his mother. She pulls a handkerchief out of her pocket, wipes Darryl's face, puts the hankie back, and takes Darryl by the arm. She does not acknowledge Big Boss, just walks away from him with her arm around Darryl.

I have not been breathing. I realize this as I take in a gulp of air. Then suddenly I am running, pulling Clarice along. We don't stop until we are on our bus. We tear by Bernette, crash down on a seat, and hang out the window to see what's going on.

Big Boss, he's back in his truck now, and Little Boss is on his way to the truck. I know he's scared of his father, but he walks with this swagger. And as he nears the truck, he spits in the direction of Darryl and the others. They are walking fast away from school and the spit doesn't reach them, but Little Boss grins anyway. Then he walks around the front of the truck and I can't see him anymore.

Clarice and me, we sort ourselves out and decide to sit near the back of the bus. We stand up and hurry down the aisle. As we pass HRH, she snorts at me and says, "Piggy, piggy."

I smile sweetly. "Why, thank you," I reply.

Finally the bus rolls off and I lean back in my seat. Clarice is looking sleepy. It has been a day.

And I have some thinking to do about Ray Stomper, Jr. Like, do I really want to be his friend?

Six

I half expected the school bus to be noisy on the way home. Bernette, I think she expected it too. But we are so quiet that she looks concerned. She keeps glancing in the rearview mirror at us kids as she hauls the bus through Coker Creek and around our hills. Clarice is not the only one asleep. And the kids who are awake are just staring out the windows. I don't know about them, but I am thinking about Darryl and Little Boss and Big Boss and the spitting and the parents. Today wasn't near as bad as Little Rock, but it wasn't what I expected either.

The spitting is so horrible that I can't think about

it for too long. It seems to me that when a thought or a memory is especially awful, my brain rejects it after a while. I want to note this in my journal. I imagine going to my room later, writing in my journal, and starting my autobiography. Then I try to remember key points in my childhood. And then I wonder what Miss Casey will write about. Before I know it, my mind is a million miles away.

Bernette drops us kids off in the reverse order in which she picked us up, so I do not get to see where HRH Vanessa lives. I am dying to know what her house and her parents and her little brother the prince look like. All very fancy I am sure.

"Bye, Clarice," I say as Bernette flings the steering wheel around at the top of our hill, bus gears grinding. "Watch *The Edge of Night* for me."

"Oh, I will." Clarice will get home in the nick of time.

As I walk by HRH, she snorts at me again. This time I reply, "Bye, little piggy."

HRH looks startled. All she can think to say is, "You're the little piggy."

I stare at her for a moment. I am not surprised that HRH has decided to pick on me. But I am not going to let it be easy for her. "You need more practice," I tell her finally.

"At what?"

"Insults. You got a ways to go."

I hurry down the steps and hop onto the road. "See you, Bernette," I call. I run to our front porch, where Gran is sitting in the lawn chair, shelling peas. "Gran! Gran! Miss Casey is the best teacher in the world!" I exclaim.

Gran takes both of my hands in hers. "I'm glad school is off to a good start, Adele," she says.

I almost say, *"Adele?!* Who are you calling Adele? That's Mama's name." But something makes me stop. Instead I say, "Yeah, it's off to a good start. I even like tonight's homework. We each have to write our autobiography."

"Lord in heaven, what's that?" asks Gran.

"Our life story," I say grandly. "We have to tell it in two pages. It's so's Miss Casey can get to know us better. And Miss Casey, *she's* going to write *her* autobiography too. So's we can get to know her better. Did you ever hear of such a thing?"

Gran allows as how she hasn't. Then she says vaguely, "You better go round up Lyman now, honey."

Lyman is my mama's brother. He's been dead since before the thermometer broke and got stuck on forty.

I am in my room with my journal. I am trying to sort out my thoughts about Gran, about Little Boss, about Darryl, and school. If I lie on my back across my bed in the wrong direction, with my legs hanging down over the side, I can look out the window at the sky. I try to imagine Gran's God up there. Once in a picture book from the library I saw a drawing of God. He looked a little like Santa Claus — an old man with a long beard sitting on a throne in the clouds, sur- rounded by tiny angel-babies. I asked Mama about the picture and she said she didn't think God was old or young or even a man. She said she thought God was more like a presence or a feeling. I said I had heard that God is love, and she wrinkled her nose and said, "Well, maybe," and went back to her Salem cigarette.

I wonder if God has all the answers. I could use some answers today.

I sigh and get up to look at the clock in the kitchen. *The Edge of Night* is over. I am desperate to know what happened, but we don't have a telephone, so I will have to wait until tomorrow when Clarice will fill me in on the bus. I put away my journal, open my notebook, and begin my autobiography.

That night Mama is home again in time for dinner. I wish Mr. Titus would make up his mind about the double shifts, but I am glad to see Mama. I am about to tell her what went on in school when she says, "Guess what. I have good news."

I freeze. Mama's good news is sometimes only good for Mama. Like the time her good news was that she had taken a job in Fort Hall and would only be home on weekends.

Mama lifts her glass of Coke to her lips and I notice that she has painted her nails orange. "I," she says, proud-like, "am going to be attending secretarial school."

"Really?" I cry.

"Adele!" exclaims Gran. She sounds pleased, but then she adds, "How . . . ?"

I know she means, "How can we afford it?"

Mama hesitates just slightly, then fumbles for her Salems before remembering Gran's feelings about smoking in the kitchen. "Well, I took out a tiny loan at the bank. *Very* tiny," she says. "I'll be able to pay it back in no time once I have a good secretarial job in Mechanicsville or somewheres. And also, I used a teeny bit of the school money."

There is silence at the table. The school money is so's I can go to college one day. It is money that we have scrimped and saved for. Gran, she has sold our chickens' eggs, and Mama, if she has had an extra dollar here or there . . . all that has gone into the jar of school money, and every time the jar gets full, we take the money to the bank and put it in the school account. But, I think, college is a long ways away. I'm only ten now. Surely, if Mama has a good secretarial job she can pay the money back before I'm ready for college. Plus, school is school. Why should it matter whether it's Mama or me who's going?

"Mama, I'm proud of you," I tell her.

"Thank you, precious." Mama looks proud of herself, which is nice.

Gran is still looking worried. "When are you going to *go* to school?" she wants to know. "How are you going to fit it in with the double shifts and all?"

"Well, I talked to Mr. Titus, and now I am pretty sure I will only have to work days. School is at night.

Three nights a week. If we need extra money, I can find something for the other nights. Bartending at the Lantern, maybe."

"They need somebody there again?" asks Gran at the same time I say, "When are you going to do your homework?"

Mama shrugs. I can tell she has not thought her plan all the way through. We will just have to see what happens.

Gran turns to me. "Belle Teal, how was school today?"

I tell myself that Gran is asking this for Mama's benefit, since Gran already knows darn well how school was today. On the other hand, I didn't tell her anything about Darryl and the colored children, and maybe that is what she is asking about.

I put my thoughts in order. I try to tell Gran and Mama everything that happened, from seeing the parents at school when I got off the bus, to Darryl's arrival, to Big Boss and Little Boss and the spitting.

"I was scared of those parents," I say finally. "They sounded so angry."

"But not at you," says Mama.

"I know. They're angry at Darryl and the others."

"I don't know as they're angry at them," Mama says slowly, "so much as —"

"They sound like they hate them," I interrupt her.

"Well . . ."

"Why?"

Mama sighs and fiddles around again for her cigarettes. "I suppose they think the colored children shouldn't mix with their white children."

"They think they're better than them just because they're white," I say, and feel heat rising to my face. I realize I'm not scared after all. I'm angry. I'm angry like those parents. Angry *at* the parents. I think of the spitting. I'm angry at Little Boss too.

I am trying to settle down when Gran says, "Well, Belle Teal. The first day of school. How did it go?"

I am dumbfounded. I stand up in a rush, sending my chair crashing into the wall behind me. "I have to write my stupid autobiography, that's how it went," I say, and stomp off.

By bedtime I have finished the autobiography, and I know it isn't stupid. It is two and half pages long, though, and I hope Miss Casey won't mind. Some teachers, when they say something they really mean it. They won't give an inch. I don't know much about Miss Casey yet, but I have a feeling she won't mind an extra half page. Besides, I have worked really hard, and I think what I have written is good. I am reading it over one more time when Mama comes into my room.

"Did you wash your hair yet, precious?" she asks me.

My hair is not wet and I have a feeling I look like a pigpen, so Mama's question annoys me.

"No," I say.

"Get up half an hour early tomorrow then, and you can do it in the morning. It's bedtime now."

"Okay."

Suddenly I feel like a very little girl again. When Mama sits down on my bed I lean into her and she strokes my hair. "Precious," she says, "my classes start next week. If I do get a job at the Lantern I won't be home much at all. You and Gran will be on your own."

I nod. "Yeah."

"So you take care of each other, okay? Can you do that?"

Now Gran, she has always taken care of me. And of the house and the chickens and the garden. I wonder what it is Mama wants me to do for Gran, beyond what I already do, which is generally help out with things.

"You want me to take on more chores?" I ask. I won't mind doing that. Mama's education is important.

"No. Just help Gran with remembering . . . what to do."

"Mama, what's wrong with Gran these days?" I move away from Mama so's I can look at her face.

"Oh, she's just getting old, precious."

I think that Mama, who's gazing across my room, is looking a little old herself.

Seven

On the way to school the next morning, I make up my mind. I am going to say something to Little Boss about the spitting. Big Boss can be as mean as he wants, but if Little Boss is going to follow in his daddy's footsteps, then he is going to have to deal with me.

Clarice and me are sitting near the back of the bus again. Clarice has already filled me in on *The Edge of Night* and now she is looking ahead in our fifth-grade reader, sneaking a peek at the tall tales we will be studying later. In the front of the bus, in the very first seat, is HRH, the Supreme Goddess of Everything, wearing a different skirt-and-sweater set. This one is pink, and Lord, I hate to admit it, but it is the exact color of strawberry ice cream, and if we could ever afford a skirt-and-sweater set for me, that is probably the one I would want, although I am usually not one for pink.

I myself am wearing the same outfit I had on yesterday. Gran, she looked so sorry when she said this, but she told me I would have to make do with the green shift until the next day when she could get around to letting out the hems on the two skirts from fourth grade that I can still wear. She said maybe on the weekend she and Mama and I can run over to Mechanicsville and look through the clothing rack at Woolworth's. I am hoping that the Sears catalog will arrive in the meantime, since there is nothing I like less than trying on clothes. Anyway, what I really want is a new pair of boots, ones that won't pinch my toes.

HRH has turned around in her seat, and her eyes have glommed on to me. What is she staring at? I took a bath and washed my hair this morning, so I am as fine as I am going to get.

I concentrate on what to say to Little Boss. He is a funny one. Threats don't usually work with him. But once last year when I had had enough of him, I told him I wasn't going to be his friend anymore, and right away he stopped teasing Clarice about her new glasses.

The bus pulls up in front of Coker Creek Elementary, and I realize I am holding my breath, waiting to see what those parents are up to.

"Look," I say to Clarice as Bernette brings the bus to a stop. I am pointing to the walk in front of school, where only four parents are standing, and only one of them has a sign. I guess they have gotten the message that Darryl and the others are here to stay.

"But look at *that*," replies Clarice.

I feel my stomach turn over when I see Big Boss sitting in his pickup by himself. Just sitting.

"I wonder if Darryl is here yet." I scan the kids who are walking into school, but I don't see him.

Clarice and me, we step off the bus and run by Big Boss's truck as fast as we can. We have already reached the front doors of the school when we hear a commotion behind us. I dare to turn around and look. There's Big Boss yelling and banging on the sides of the pickup with his bare hands.

Darryl has arrived. He's with his mother again, along with the other two colored kids and their mothers. Because of where Big Boss is parked, the six of them have to walk by his truck. Either that or walk across the school lawn, which is not allowed, and I do not think they are going to break any rules. So they look straight ahead and just keep walking.

Big Boss starts swearing to beat the band. I think maybe he has had something to drink.

"Where's Little Boss?" Clarice whispers to me as we run inside.

I shake my head.

We reach the door with the yellow paper sun taped to it and hurry to our desks. I see Little Boss standing at the windows, looking out at the pickup truck, and his eyes, they are so confused. Maybe even a little sad. I almost forget about the speech I have planned for him. But then I remember the spitting, and decide to go ahead with it. I grab his elbow and pull him to the back of the room.

"Little Boss, if I ever see you spit at Darryl or anyone again —" I start to say.

"Yeah?" Little Boss sticks out his jaw, defiant.

"Then I'm not . . ." I almost can't say it. "I won't be your friend anymore. And I mean it."

"What are you, some kind of ni —" Little Boss stops himself.

"I mean it," I say again.

"All right." He jerks his elbow away and stalks across the room to Chas and Vernon.

The parents with the picket signs give up pretty quickly and go home. Not long after, Big Boss leaves too. I am pleased. Now I can give my full attention to what is written on the blackboard. It is Miss Casey's own personal autobiography.

"I will read yours in private," she tells us. "You may have shared things with me that you didn't intend for the entire class to see. But I want you to get to know me, so I have copied my autobiography on the board for you to read. I'll leave it there until the end of the day. Feel free to read it whenever you have a moment."

Reading Miss Casey's autobiography, that is the highlight of my day, maybe even of my week. It answers a lot of questions that have been running through my brain. For instance, Miss Casey has an older brother and a younger sister, so she is a middle child. She allows as how that was not easy for her, and I could just swoon over this bare honesty. Miss Casey is twenty-six years old. She lives outside of Mechanicsville. She is not yet married and she does not have any children, although she points out that five days a week she has nineteen children. She has traveled extensively throughout the United States. She went to college in Boston, but she was born and raised in Minnesota. In my mind, that is the only disappointing part of her autobiography. That Minnesota gets to claim her. I wanted Miss Casey to be from around here, in our hills, so's we could claim her. And I do wish Miss Casey had answered the more personal questions I've been wondering about, like who her friends are and what she eats for dinner, but I understand that she couldn't cram in every little detail.

I find Miss Casey's autobiography a satisfaction.

Miss Casey, she runs things very smooth in our classroom. She is as wonderful and as sweet as I thought she would be, but she does not let us get away with a thing. Which is why nobody, not even Chas or Vernon or Little Boss, says one mean word to Darryl. 'Course, nobody says one nice word to him either, but this is only his second day here. I myself am storing up lots of things I want to ask him when the time seems right.

At the end of our second day in school, three of

the parents show up to hoot and howl at the colored kids and their folks. And Big Boss, he's sitting in his truck again. I make a point of walking outside with Little Boss. I walk him as close to the pickup as I dare, and I give him a couple of pinches in his side to remind him about the talk we had in the morning. Little Boss glares at me and looks put out, but he does not say anything to Darryl and the others.

When our third day of school begins, the only parent hanging around in front of the school is Big Boss in his truck. And today, he will not leave. An hour goes by and he is still sitting there, staring at the school building and smoking. Another hour goes by, then a third. I can tell he's making Little Boss nervous. And Miss Casey, she keeps glancing out the window at him. Eventually, she excuses herself from our room. A few minutes after she comes back, I see our principal, Mr. Walter, stride along the front walk to the truck and have a chat with Big Boss. (Little Boss looks like the squirrel that accidentally got into our house last spring, and all it wanted was a good hiding place.) I am sure Big Boss will leave then. But he doesn't. He sticks around for another hour or so, to make his point. Then he leaves. He comes back at the end of the day, though, for his yelling and banging and all.

By the last day of the week, the only parent who bothers to show up is Big Boss and this time he drops Little Boss off, then drives away in a hurry.

"Got himself a job with the road crew," Little Boss tells me as we stand on the school steps.

I have a feeling Big Boss will be scarce from now on, and I am feeling happy. Until the sad thing that happens a few minutes later.

That morning HRH waltzes up to Miss Casey's desk and hands her a note. There is this smug look on HRH's face that I don't like.

Miss Casey, she reads that note and her lips tighten. The next thing I know, Vanessa and Clarice are switching seats. Now Clarice is in the front row again, next to Darryl, and Vanessa is in the third row. I wait for an explanation, but Miss Casey just takes attendance and milk orders and gets on with our day.

On the playground, me and Clarice overhear Vanessa talking to Mae.

"Well, *my* daddy just would not stand for it," HRH

is saying. "Of all things. Next to a colored boy. He called Miss Casey at home last night. Said she *had* to change my seat. He wrote her a note too, to make sure."

I look at Clarice. Then I look across the playground at Darryl. He is huddled with the two other colored kids. By now I know their names. They are Winnie and Terrence. The three of them still have to stick with a teacher for protection. Seeing that, thinking of HRH and Big Boss and the parents and their signs, all I feel is plain sad.

That is what I put in my journal that night. About Darryl and HRH and my sadness. Then I put in about Little Boss's bruise, just to get my mind on something else. Lordy, he came into school with a big one this morning. On his arm. He told me he fell off his porch. Little Boss must be the clumsiest person in the county. He fell off his porch in fourth grade too, and twice he got black eyes by walking into doors.

I feel the need for adding something happier to my journal, so I write that Gran is already thinking ahead to our Christmas fruitcakes, which we make every year on the day after Thanksgiving. This gets me to thinking about the holidays, starting with Halloween. I look outside and see a V of geese silhouetted against a full moon. I hear them honking as they make their way south for the winter. And I feel a little chill, like all of a sudden autumn has come upon us.

Eight

I am putting my milk money in my purse necklace, and Gran, she is at the sink with the breakfast dishes. Under her breath she is singing something about "coming in on a wing and a prayer."

Mama bustles into the kitchen in her spanking clean Adele uniform. She gives Gran a quick peck on the cheek. "I'm off," she says. She gulps some coffee.

"You do your homework, Mama?" I ask.

"Yeah, precious. You?"

"All done."

I like that Mama and I both have homework to

do. The two of us have been in school for a month now, and Mama has not missed a class *or* a day of work. She has done every one of her secretarial assignments too. (She is showing me how to make her shorthand squiggles.) From time to time she fills in at the Lantern. All in all, I think the money from the school account is being well spent.

I have done every one of my homework assignments too, but then, I always do. Besides, I would not want to disappoint Miss Casey. An A or a star or a *Well done!* from her makes my insides feel glorious.

Gran holds a plate of eggs and fried potatoes toward Mama, who waves it away. "I don't have time," she says. "I'll be late. And I have a perfect work record so far." She wipes the coffee from her lips and flies out the door. "School tonight," she calls. "I'll be home late."

I stand up. "I better go too, Gran. The bus'll be here any minute." I give her a hug.

"You keep an eye on Lyman," Gran murmurs as I gather up my books.

I don't bother with an answer. I can hear the school bus. I tear across our yard and reach the road just as Bernette crests the top of our hill.

Autumn is getting into full swing. Here and there

I see bright spots of color in the trees. Today is misty with a raw wind. I huff out my breath, but the air isn't cold enough to make a frosty puff yet. Still, I am a bit chilly. I look down at my boots. I should have worn socks with them. I can feel the wind blowing under my cotton skirt. I am not worried, though. Today, Gran is going to set to work on a plaid flannel dress for me.

Bernette opens the door of the bus with a *whoosh*.

"Good morning," I call to her.

"Morning, honey."

I clomp up the steps and try to ignore HRH, who's wearing what looks like a brand-new cream-colored woolen dress. I can't ignore the dress, though. It looks so toasty warm. HRH's mother, she might have bought it in Paris. I wonder again what Mrs. Mathers is like. I still have not seen Vanessa's house or anything. Mrs. Mathers is probably all lovely and good-smelling, like Miss Casey. And will never have to wear a uniform with her name stitched on the pocket.

I scan the back of the bus for Clarice.

"She's not in attendance," HRH says to me, all uppity-like.

I pretend I don't know what she's talking about.

"To who are you referring?" I reply, grabbing onto the back of a seat as Bernette wheels the bus around.

"The person to *whom* I am referring is your friend Clarice."

I shrug my shoulders. "So?" I head for the back of the bus. I don't mind sitting alone. I have a fresh Nancy Drew book from the school library.

As I pass by HRH Vanessa, she starts to whistle a tune. It takes me just a moment to realize what words go with that tune. I heard them over at Clarice's. "Come and listen to a story 'bout a man named Jed, a poor mountaineer barely kept his family fed . . ."

HRH is whistling the song from this new TV show, *The Beverly Hillbillies*. I think of the Clampetts, chugging around in their hillbilly car, making fools of themselves.

I pretend I don't get her joke. "Oh, did you watch the show too?" I say, all sweet-like to HRH.

I walk toward the back and slide into a seat in front of Chas and Vernon. "Hey," we all say to each other, and then I get busy with my book. I take little peeks up at the front of the bus, though, and I see that HRH keeps turning around to look at me. I just ignore her, which nearly drives her crazy. One thing, I am sure she doesn't want anyone to think she watched *The Beverly Hillbillies,* which thanks to me now they probably do.

I am a master at not giving HRH Vanessa Mathers the time of day.

The bus pulls up in front of Coker Creek Elementary. I hold my breath, like Clarice and I have done the last several mornings. I crane my neck to see if the pickup truck is in front of school. It isn't. I let out a big sigh of relief. Just a few cars, and a couple of mothers who walk their kindergartners to school.

This makes six whole school days in a row that Big Boss hasn't shown up at Coker Creek to curse and shout. Even after he got the job with the road crew he would show up once a week or so. But I think he has given up for good now.

It appears that I am not the only one who thinks so. Lordy, I wish Clarice was here so I could share this particular piece of news with her: I am looking out the bus window and I am not seeing Big Boss, but I *am* seeing Darryl and Winnie and Terrence, who are walking along the path to the front door of our school. They are in a tight group with their arms linked together. And their parents are not with them. They have walked to school by themselves. They look terrified, and I wonder if I could be as brave as they are.

Bernette opens the bus door and I make my way down the aisle. HRH, she is still sitting in her seat at the front. Why isn't she getting off the bus? I wonder. She turns around and sees me heading toward her.

"Oink, oink," she snorts as I pass.

Now, I don't especially like being oinked at, but it doesn't bother me all that much. Not the oinking itself. What bothers me is that HRH feels the *need* to oink at me. I step out of the aisle and wait in the seat across from Vanessa's. When everyone has left the bus, I sit there and stare at HRH.

"What are you looking at?" she asks.

"What do you think? I'm looking at you."

HRH makes a face. "Why?"

"Because I thought maybe you didn't have enough time to finish oinking at me. You oink nearly every time we're on the bus. So why don't you just go ahead and finish the job? Oh. Maybe you need an audience." I lean out of the bus. "Hey, Chas! Vernon! Come back here." I turn to Bernette. "This'll just take a minute," I tell her.

When Chas and Vernon have stuck their heads in

the bus, I say to HRH, "Okay. Go on." I look back at the boys. "Vanessa didn't finish oinking at me," I tell them. "And she wanted you to hear her. Go ahead, Vanessa."

Well, Vanessa, now she doesn't say a word. And the boys are smirking at her.

"Come on. We're going to be late," I say to HRH. "Oink, oink. Snort, snort. Come *on*."

One small part of me thinks HRH might start to cry. She doesn't. She rolls her eyes, pushes her way past Chas and Vernon, and flounces off the bus.

Maybe the oinking will stop. Maybe it won't. But I think I've gotten under HRH's skin.

In the cafeteria that day I buy my milk and sit down at the table where me and Clarice always sit. Occasionally we sit with Chas and Vernon and Little Boss, once in a while with Kayla, who stopped sitting with HRH after the first day of school. But the boys are with other boys today, and Kayla, I don't even see her. So I am settling down at the table all by myself when I see Darryl. I guess he's on his way to sit with Winnie and Terrence. As he passes by me I smile at him and say, "Hey, Darryl."

At first, Darryl, he looks alarmed. But then he smiles back. "Hey, Belle Teal," he answers.

I've got that glorious feeling inside me.

The next day turns out to be something, all right. One thing, HRH didn't oink at me on the bus the previous afternoon, and she doesn't oink this morning either. She makes quite a face, though. When she does I give her one of my big grins. Another thing, Clarice is absent again, and I notice Chas isn't on the bus either. A huge cold is going around, which I haven't caught yet.

When we get to Coker Creek Elementary it turns out that half the school is absent. Including Winnie and Terrence. Darryl walks to school all by himself and I feel bad for him. He comes hurrying along so fast, it's like a Halloween monster is after him. He hightails it into our classroom in record time.

At lunch that day I am by myself again. And so is Darryl. Well, this is just silly, I think. So I pick up my milk carton and my lunch bag and I walk to Darryl's table and I just sit down across from him.

"Hey," I say. Darryl nearly chokes on his sandwich and I don't blame him. "Clarice is absent," I tell him.

Darryl, he coughs and nods.

"Do you mind if I sit here?"

Darryl shakes his head. "No."

Darryl's lunch and mine are about the same. Sandwich, apple, cookie, school milk. Except my cookie is oatmeal and Darryl's is chocolate chip.

I break my cookie in two pieces. "Want half?" I ask. I hold one piece out to Darryl.

Darryl breaks his cookie in two and holds one piece out to me. "I'll trade you," he answers.

Darryl's cookie is so good, they should make TV commercials about it. I tell him so.

"Thanks," he says. "My mother made it. Yours is good too."

"My gran made it."

After that we eat our sandwiches without talking. Some kids have turned around at other tables and are staring at us, but I won't look back at them. I concentrate on my lunch.

Finally I say, "I live with my mom and my gran. Gran, she's a really good cook. She does all our cooking. Every year she makes our Thanksgiving dinner. And then on the day after Thanksgiving, she and Mama and me make Christmas fruitcakes." I pause. "But my mama is a horrible cook."

Darryl grins. "My mother's not so good either. Except for cookies. She burns everything. But my aunt is really good."

"Your aunt who lives next door?"

"Yeah. How did you know?"

"You told us. On the first day of school when you introduced yourself."

"And you remembered?"

"Yeah. Hey, Darryl, the hospital where your mother works, is it Baptist Memorial? Because I had my appendix out there and maybe I met her." Before Darryl has a chance to answer me, I go on, "And what is a machinist? I've been wondering."

Darryl and I start talking and we can't stop. We finish our lunches and we're still talking. Then we go out to the playground and keep right on talking. Gran says I could talk the ear off a stalk of corn, and I have nearly a month's worth of questions stored up, and Darryl, it turns out he's quite a talker himself, even if he is on the shy side.

I can't wait for Clarice to feel better so she can get to know Darryl too.

When the bell rings and it's time to line up to go back to our classrooms, HRH oinks at both Darryl and me. Darryl backs away from her, but I stand nose to nose with her and say, "Okay, finish up, Vanessa. We'll stay right here. Come on, I know you're not done yet."

Vanessa looks disgusted and walks away from us.

Darryl stares at me.

"You just have to know how to handle her," I tell him.

Nine

That cold bug keeps Clarice out of school for two more days. It keeps Winnie and Terrence out for one more day. On the day they come back, they sit with Darryl at their usual table in the cafeteria. So I sit by myself. I have just bitten into my peanut butter sandwich when someone slides into the empty chair across from me.

"Hey," says Darryl.

"Hey!" I say. I look across the noisy room at Terrence and Winnie, then back at Darryl. "Don't you want to sit with them?" I ask.

"I see them all the time. It's okay." Darryl grins.

"You sure?"

"Yup."

So Darryl and me, we eat our lunches together. Later, on the playground, I notice a kid, I think it's Kayla's younger brother Jeremy, playing Four Square with Terrence and Winnie. Darryl and me decide to play with them for a while, but then we lapse away and just start talking again. I think Darryl doesn't want to all the time be stuck with fourth-graders, even if they are colored like him.

When Clarice finally returns to school, her eyes are red and streamy, and she is still blowing her nose. She keeps a tissue tucked up her sleeve at all times. But she says she is better. It's been so long since I've seen her that I'm more of a chatterbox than ever on the bus that morning. I tell her about HRH and the oinking, and then she wants to catch me up on *The Edge of Night,* but I am dying to move on to the most important topic, which is Darryl.

"We have been sitting together in the cafeteria," I report. I tell her about our conversations, and about Terrence and Winnie. "You will really like Darryl. There is not a mean bone in his body," I add, quoting Gran. "Unlike Chas and Little Boss and Vernon's bodies."

That day, Darryl and Clarice and me eat lunch together. Now Clarice, when she doesn't buy cafeteria food, the inside of her lunch box is like a market. She has crackers and a brownie and a hard-boiled egg and two pieces of fruit and some cheese cubes and some nuts and even spaghetti and meatballs in a container. She eats the spaghetti with an actual fork her mother has rolled up inside a paper napkin.

Clarice's lunch is great for trading. She grins when she sees that Darryl has one of his cookies, which I have told her how good they are, and she trades him the brownie *and* the egg for it. I get the crackers and cheese cubes for just half of my sandwich.

Once all the trading has settled down, Clarice, she mentions *The Beverly Hillbillies* and Darryl, he says, "You have a TV?" His whole face has lit up. "You ever watch *Bonanza?*"

"A couple of times," says Clarice, and then they are off and running about *Bonanza.*

Little Boss walks by our table then and whomps into the back of Darryl's chair, making Darryl spill his milk.

"Hey!" I cry, but Little Boss walks on without looking back. I can't tell if it was an accident or not. "Little Boss, you come back here!"

"Ignore him, Belle Teal," says Clarice. She opens her Thermos and pours some juice into a Dixie cup and pushes it across the table to Darryl. "Here," she says. "Have this instead." Darryl and Clarice, they go back to their conversation about *Bonanza*.

On the playground that day, after Clarice has tried to explain *The Edge of Night* to Darryl, the three of us decide to make up our own drama. It is about three people in New York City, where none of us has ever been. Darryl wants to play a fireman in the drama, Clarice decides to be a movie star, and I am a struggling writer. Our characters all happen to live in the same apartment building. We call our drama *City Lights,* since we live in one of those lit-up skyscrapers like the Empire State Building, and I think our show is very good. We will make up our lines, which I will write down and then we will act them out.

Once or twice Darryl, he looks over at Terrence and Winnie, but they are playing Four Square again, this time with Jeremy and his friend Will. Four Square doesn't hold much appeal for us writers.

"Let's work on our drama every day," says Clarice, and Darryl and me agree that this is a very good idea.

When school ends that day, Clarice and me and Darryl walk outside together. Darryl meets up with Winnie and Terrence, and we say good-bye to him.

"Hey, Belle Teal! Clarice!" calls someone from behind us.

We turn around and there is Little Boss with Vernon and Chas.

Right away, I sense trouble. "What," I say, flat-like.

"Well, we were just wondering," Little Boss starts to say. "What is in that colored boy's lunch box every day? Fried chicken and watermelon?"

"That boy has a name," I reply, "and it is Darryl."

Little Boss ignores this. "So are you eating colored food for lunch now?"

I draw in a great big breath. I have to stop and think of Gran and her gentle ways and her belief in the Lord. Also, I look at the fresh bruise under Little Boss's left eye.

Finally I just say, "No." Then I take Clarice by the elbow and lead her to our bus, where I choose one of the seats in the very first row. This means we will have to sit across the aisle from HRH Vanessa Mathers. But I would rather do that than sit within ten feet of Chas and Vernon.

The month of October is rushing by like the yellow leaves outside my bedroom window. Miss Casey has increased our homework little by little, but she makes up for it by reading aloud to us for twenty minutes every day after recess. Last week she started *The Big Wave,* by Pearl S. Buck, and when I listen to it I feel almost as breathless as when Sarah Lane Karr died on *The Edge of Night.* Miss Casey, she is a pure wonder.

One morning, about two weeks before Halloween, Miss Casey stands in front of our room holding a piece of chalk in one hand and *The Big Wave* in the other. She asks us to think about the stories she has been reading to us, and also about the little compositions we have written ourselves. I sit very still in my chair. I frown up my eyebrows. What, exactly, does Miss Casey want us to think when we think about our compositions? I try to remember the names of mine: "The Last Firefly," "Autumn in Our Hills," "The Lonesome Hound."

Then, to my great surprise, Miss Casey, she says, "I believe it is time for you to write your own books."

Our own books? Lord above, I am not ready for that.
"There are some fine writers in our class," Miss
Casey continues. "And some fine artists. I am going to
assign you to work in pairs. Each pair will make a sto-
rybook, complete with illustrations and a cover, to
share with your classmates."

I am overjoyed except for that part about being
assigned to work in pairs. I know teachers and they
are famous for matching up two people who don't get
along in order to make them get along. I am certain to
be paired with HRH Vanessa.

Miss Casey puts down the book and the chalk and
picks up a piece of paper from her desk. When she
moves, her perfume from France wafts all the way
over to my desk, and I breathe it in and hold on to it
for good luck.

Miss Casey starts reading off pairs of names. Vernon is paired with poor Stephen. Clarice is paired
with Mae. Now I am certain I am to be paired with
HRH. I am trying to figure out how we could write
our story without ever having to talk to each other,
when I hear Miss Casey, say, "Belle Teal." Inside my
desk, I cross my fingers.

Then Miss Casey, she says, "Darryl."

I let out my breath. I can't believe it! I turn my head to grin at Darryl. He is grinning back at me.

I love Miss Casey. I really do.

When she tells us to break into our pairs and start talking about our books, me and Darryl huddle up in the back of the room.

"You can draw all the pictures!" I say.

"And you can write out the story," says Darryl. "But we'll make it up together."

We are experts at making up stories by now, what with our work on *City Lights,* which we get to whenever we can. So far, we have written and acted out eight episodes. But our book, we decide, will not be another daytime drama. It will be a Halloween tale of some type.

When I get home from school that afternoon I make a beeline for my journal. I have to write in it immediately. Because of what happened on the bus.

It was Vernon who said it. As me and Clarice slid into our regular seat, Vernon leaned forward and hissed into my ear. "Nigger-lovers," he said. Then he leaned back with his arms folded and glared at me.

I faced forward and just stared straight ahead. I could not answer him.

I don't like what he said, and I sure don't like how he said it.

I write this in my journal. What I really want to do is talk to Mama or Gran about it. But Mama is at work cleaning rooms at the R U Sleep Inn, and Gran, well, it does feel like I'm the one looking after her now, instead of the other way around. One thing, she hardly ever seems to know how to dress to go outside anymore. And not just because of the stuck thermometer. She appears to have forgotten about her special way of reading the weather. Sometimes she goes outside with three sweaters on when the temperature is creeping up on seventy. Sometimes the opposite. No jacket and it's not even forty. And Gran is *so* forgetful. Still, our meals are always cooked and the house seems about as clean as ever. Not as sparkly as on some TV commercials, but tidy enough. The yard looks a little scraggly, but then there's not much to do at this time of year. Still . . . Gran is not one for conversations lately. Mostly she putters around and sings little songs under her breath.

I look down at what I have written in my journal. I see "I HATE VERNON." I pick up my pencil and erase that. "Hate just creates more hate," Mama said. And she is right.

Ten

On the morning of October 17, I wake up as a thought springs into my head: Just two weeks to Halloween, and I don't have any idea about my costume. Every year I make my own. A lot of kids buy theirs. I have seen the stacks of costume boxes on the shelf near the cash register at Sherman's in Coker Creek. On each box is a picture of the costume — Frankenstein, a gypsy, a devil, a cat, a princess, a skeleton — and inside is a plastic mask or a cloth hood and a little suit you can slip into. Gran says we can't be paying for foolishness like that, and I am glad. The fun of Halloween is dreaming up a costume and then figuring out how to make it. Last year I was a caboose and I turned a cardboard box into a train car and wore it around my middle. Gran said, "My land, Belle Teal. I have never seen anything like it before."

At lunch I ask Clarice and Darryl if they know what they are going to wear to our school Halloween party. Clarice says, "I have no idea. Maybe I'll be a fox."

"How are you going to be a fox?" I ask her.

Clarice shrugs. Our fourth-grade teacher wrote on Clarice's report card that Clarice needs to work on carrying out her ideas.

Darryl, he looks uncomfortable. "I'm not sure I'm going to come to the party."

"But Darryl, you have to come. It's the best school party of the year," I tell him. "Except for the Christmas program."

Darryl is fiddling with his straw paper. "It's at night, isn't it?"

"Of course," Clarice replies. "You can't have a Halloween party in the daylight."

"No . . ."

We finish our lunches and go out to the playground. Instead of working on *City Lights,* Clarice and me spend all of recess telling Darryl how wonderful the Halloween party is. The three of us just huddle up and talk. By the time the bell rings and we are standing on line, I think we have pretty much convinced Darryl to go. "I could be a fireman," he says. "I even have a red fireman's hat."

So that is the good thing. The bad thing is that as Clarice and me are about to get on our bus that afternoon, Vernon calls us that name again.

The way he hisses the words makes them sound even dirtier than they already are.

A funny look travels across Clarice's face. Then she marches up the steps of the bus and says to Bernette as we walk by, "Belle Teal is coming home with me this afternoon, so you can skip driving up the hill."

Bernette looks awful relieved, not to mention HRH, who has overheard Clarice. But I grab the back of Clarice's jacket and say, "What are you doing?"

When Clarice doesn't answer me right away, I can tell this is one of those things that she is not sure how she's going to carry it out.

"You'll see," she says as she flumps down in a seat. Bernette drives straight into Coker Creek, and at the second stop, Clarice, me, Chas, Vernon, and two other kids get off. The door of the bus has barely closed when Clarice plants herself in front of Vernon and just stands there.

"What," says Vernon.

"Say it again," says Clarice. "Call me and Belle Teal what you've been calling us."

I am shocked. I have never seen Clarice do something like this.

Vernon allows a small smile to twitch his mouth up. "Why? Are you going to fight me?" he asks. He raises his fists to Clarice's face.

Clarice looks uncertain. So I step in. "Only if you want to fight a girl," I tell him.

Now Vernon looks uncertain. He drops his fists, but he says, "Okay. Niggerloversniggerloversniggerlovers."

"My father —" Clarice starts to say, but her face just crumples.

I am feeling all cool and calm. "Vernon," I say. And then I add, "Chas," since Chas is hovering behind him. "Clarice and me are friends with Darryl and you better get used to it."

"Your *friend*," replies Vernon, "doesn't belong in *our* school."

Chas steps around Vernon, feeling braver. "And we shouldn't have to associate with his kind," he says.

"But it's okay for them to serve you meals?" I ask, knowing that Chas sometimes eats at the counter in Sherman's. The heat is rising to my face and I have to take in deep breaths and remember again about Gran and her Lord, and Mama and what she believes in.

"That's all they're good for," says Chas. "That and cleaning up."

My head begins to pound and I am about to forget everything I just tried to remember. I pull back my arm and I really think I am going to sock one of the boys, but then I drop my hand to my side and turn my back on all of them. I just march down the road toward Route 518, even though I can hear Clarice calling after me. When she calls louder, I start to run, and I keep running until I don't hear anything. Then I slow down.

Tears have come to my eyes and I blink, blink, blink all furious-like as I stomp along. I don't bother to wave in at Miss Wanda as I stomp by her beauty salon. I am breathing hard and my chest hurts. I swipe at my tears with my hand, which is none too clean. Chas and Vernon are pigs, I think. And Clarice, I could just wring her neck. How is it that Darryl doesn't go home from school in this state every single day? I wonder. Or maybe he does, and I just don't know about it.

I reach 518, blast across the highway, and hit our dirt road, which is muddy from a rainfall we had yesterday. I look up and see the trees against the sky. The leaves are starting to blow off. And that sky, it is a deep dark blue. The days are so much shorter now. By Halloween, we will have turned our clocks backward and it will be full-on dark by the time we get to school for the party.

I clomp along in my old boots, which Gran has said I will have to make do with this year if my toes can possibly take it. I hate trudging up our hill in the dark. I'm not even making good use of my thinking time. I have to concentrate so as not to trip over rocks or roots. Even so, I fall twice. The second time I go down on my knee and muddy up the flannel dress Gran just made.

By the time I fling open our front door I am a mess. I'm all muddy, my knee is bleeding, and I know I look like I've been crying.

"My stars," murmurs Gran when she sees me. "What on earth?"

I can't help myself. I start to sob.

Gran, she folds me into her arms, hums a tuneless tune.

Finally I pull away from her, look into her eyes, and say, "I think I put a hole in my dress."

"Well, never you mind. Tell me what happened, Lyman. Not fighting again, I hope." Gran has turned away and is sorting through a kitchen cupboard for Band-Aids and the Mercurochrome.

I can't answer her. The color glides out of my face, and I begin to shake.

Gran returns, takes my hand, feels the trembling, and sits me on a kitchen chair to take care of my knee.

I lean into Gran's soft, creased face and whisper, "Vernon called me a nigger-lover."

But Gran is singing softly about bluebirds and the White Cliffs of Dover and Jimmy sleeping in his own little room again, and I don't know as she has heard me. When she is satisfied with the state of my knee, she holds my hand for a moment, brushes the hair from my face, then turns to the pots on the stove.

Mama comes home late that night, long after I have turned out my light. Sometimes she goes to a study room at the secretarial school to do her homework so's to be sure she is ready for her next class. I call to her when I hear her pass by my bedroom door.

"Precious?" Mama replies. "You all right? Not sick, are you?" Mama sits on the edge of my bed and feels my forehead.

"I'm okay." The entire time I was trudging up our hill this afternoon, crying and bleeding and mad as a hornet, all I wanted to do was talk to Mama about Little Boss spitting, and those dirty words spewing out of Vernon's lips. But now, with Mama at my side, stroking my hair, what I say is, "Tell me what is really wrong with Gran. I know it's something more than just getting old. It's like she's gotten lost."

"Did something happen today?" Mama wants to know.

I tell her what Vernon said, and how Gran thought I was Lyman coming home after a fight. "Mama, Gran calls me Lyman half the time and Adele the rest of the time. Yesterday she was wearing a sweater *underneath* her dress. And she forgot Halloween is coming. I showed her the black cat and the pumpkin I made in art and she said something like it was a funny time of year for that."

The light from the kitchen creeps through the

open door to my room and falls on Mama's tired face. The corners of her mouth twitch, but not like Vernon's did in the afternoon. Mama purses her lips. She blinks her eyes. At last she says, "Precious, sometimes when people are old their minds go funny. I think maybe Gran is getting senile."

"But she's still cooking and all," I point out. "And she talked about the fruitcakes this morning. Even though she forgot Halloween."

Mama nods. "We'll just have to be patient with her. She can't help it when she forgets things. Doesn't even know she's doing it."

I lie back on my pillow. When Mama leaves the room I make my mind run away from thoughts of Gran and Vernon and Chas. I focus in on Halloween. My costume. Maybe this year I will be something beautiful. A genie, the sort who would wisp out of a bottle. I could wear some of Mama's makeup and wind my hair up on top of my head. I could look magical and mysterious and very, very wise.

Eleven

After our fight with Chas and Vernon I am mad at Clarice almost until recess the next day. On the bus in the morning, the boys make crying noises at me and pretend to wipe away tears, even though I know I did not actually cry in front of them. I don't sit near them, and I don't sit near Clarice either. I sit across the aisle from HRH and ignore all of them by reading another Nancy Drew mystery.

At lunch I sit with Clarice and Darryl as usual, but I do not speak to Clarice or trade anything with her. When she tries to talk to me, I answer like, "Darryl, please tell Clarice I do not care for her pear."

After I have done this three or four times, Darryl, he says, "Belle Teal, tell me, how long is this going to go on? I am not going to carry your messages forever."

I think for a moment. Finally I say, "It is going to stop now. But Clarice, please do not do things like that without telling me first. I have to be prepared."

"What did Clarice do?" asks Darryl.

Clarice and me look at each other. Since I am still a little mad at her I say, "Do you want to tell Darryl?"

"No," she says, annoyed-like. But then she turns to Darryl and her eyes look kind. "We had a misunderstanding, is all." She turns back to me. "Belle Teal, I am sorry for what I did."

"Well, I am sorry too."

Even so, we don't say anything for a while. Finally Darryl, he can't take the silence any longer. "I decided to come to the Halloween party," he announces.

"You did?!" Clarice and I cry.

"Are Winnie and Terrence coming?" I ask.

"Are you still going to be a fireman?" asks Clarice.

"I don't know about Winnie and Terrence," says Darryl. "And my costume —"

Darryl is interrupted when Little Boss, who has

been sitting at a table directly behind him, tips his chair backward and bumps into Darryl, squeezing his chest against the edge of our table.

"What was that you just said?" asks Little Boss.

"Little Boss, you say you're sorry!" I exclaim.

Little Boss crashes his chair back into position, then stands by Darryl's side. He is joined by Chas and Vernon.

"You," he says quiet-like to Darryl, but it's mean quiet, not kind quiet, "better not come to the party."

"This is not a party for your people," adds Vernon.

"You have already poisoned our school, you are not going to poison —" Little Boss is saying when suddenly someone else is at Darryl's side.

It's Miss Casey.

"Ray Stomper," she says, "let me remind you of something. You too, Chas and Vernon. Darryl is a student at Coker Creek and he has as much right to attend a school party as you do. Do you understand me?"

"Yes, ma'am," the boys mutter.

Miss Casey, she stands at the end of our table until the boys have settled back in their seats.

Meanwhile, I am getting an idea. But I wait until

me and Clarice and Darryl are off by ourselves on the playground before I say anything about it. Then the idea about bursts out of my mouth.

"Guess what," I say. And then I go on and tell them. "I just got an idea." I am so excited that my voice is a little trembly. "Darryl, what if everyone knew what costumes you and me were going to wear to the party, and then on Halloween night, we *switched* them. Little Boss and them, they would spend the evening with me, I mean they would think it was me but it would really be you, and then at the end of the party we would throw off our costumes and Little Boss and Vernon and Chas would see that they had played games and all with *you*. They would be so surprised! And *then* they would know that you are not poison or anything — just another kid at the party."

While I have been talking, Darryl's eyes have been growing bigger and bigger. But he doesn't say anything, so I ask him what does he think.

"Oh, Belle Teal. I — I can't do that."

"Why not?"

"Well, Little Boss would just about kill me."

"No, he wouldn't. You all will be at the party. He

couldn't do anything to you in front of everyone. You haven't been to the party before, Darryl, but some parents come too. It isn't only for kids. There'll be plenty of grown-ups there." I look at Clarice. "Don't you think it would be fun?" I ask her.

Clarice makes a face like she isn't sure. Finally she says, "Darryl, I don't think anything would happen to you. Plus, it will be our chance to make a point with the boys after everything they've been saying. But Belle Teal, how are you going to make this work? One thing, you won't be able to say a word all night long. People can tell your voices apart, you know."

"Oh, we can figure that out," I reply.

Clarice is still frowning. "And what makes you think the boys are going to want to spend time with us at the party, anyway? We just had a fight with Vernon and Chas."

"They'll get over it. They always do," I say. Us and the boys are enemy-friends. Sometimes I think even their meanest teasing is because secretly they like us. And also because practically nobody else in our class will pay them any mind.

Darryl, he says then, "I still don't have a good feeling about this."

"Darryl," I reply. "Think of every darn thing those boys have said since the very first day of school. All you are going to do is show them how they are wrong in their thinking. And I'll be doing it with you."

A teeny smile is appearing on Darryl's face. He has changed his mind around, I know it. So before he changes it back, I rush on with things. "Now, we will also have to make sure our costumes cover every inch of our bodies," I say. Our skin can't show anywhere. What could we be?"

The three of us sit down under a tree to think. By the time the bell rings we do not have a lick of an idea, but we like our plan better and better. We are going to teach those boys a lesson.

It takes us several days of thinking and talking under the tree at recess before we smooth out our plan. The first costume we decide on is a devil for Darryl (but really for me). Clarice, she says Shari just gave her a bunch of her old Halloween costumes, the ones from Sherman's. The oldest is a devil costume and it is perfect because since devils are supposed to be all red, it comes with a red hood, so my entire head will be covered. I can add red mittens and socks to cover my hands and ankles. And I will come up with a spooky, gravelly devil voice. No one will be able to tell if it's Darryl or me talking like that.

We have to think a lot longer before we come up with a second costume. Finally one day, Darryl, he looks at me and Clarice and says like a cartoon mad scientist, "I've got it!"

"What?" I cry.

"Mickey Mouse," says Darryl.

"Mickey Mouse?" says Clarice.

"Yes. Mickey Mouse wears gloves on his hands. And he talks in a little high squeaky voice. Belle Teal and I can work on the voice until we both do it the same, just like we did for the devil voice."

"What about your head?" asks Clarice.

"I know," I say. I am just a whiz at Halloween costumes. "We can paint a big paper bag to look like Mickey's face. Darryl can wear the bag over his head."

"Hmm," says Darryl. "A paper bag . . ."

"Remember, this is supposed to be *my* costume," I say. "And it would be just like me to make a paper-bag Mickey head."

Darryl and Clarice and me look at each other.

"Well, I think it would work," says Clarice.

"All we have to do is make sure everybody knows what our costumes are going to be," I say.

Now when I think of the Halloween party I get a shivery feeling of excitement. I make sure I write up every inch of our plan in my journal.

Twelve

On Halloween morning I sneak my costume on in my room and walk into the kitchen dressed as Mickey Mouse.

"Good morning!" I say in the squeaky voice that Darryl and I have worked out.

Gran looks up from setting the table and jumps a mile. "Lord above," she says, her hand over her heart.

I whip off the paper bag head. "Gran, it's just me," I say.

Gran is not smiling. She stares at me.

I work to pull off my gloves and Mama's big old

black snow boots I hope look like Mickey's shoes. "Gran, it's me," I say again. "Today is Halloween, remember? This is my costume. We have our Halloween parade at school this afternoon, and the party tonight."

"Halloween," scoffs Gran. She turns to the stove. "Haints and ghouls . . . haints," she mutters again, and shakes her head.

"You coming to the party tonight?" I ask. "You and Mama? Mama doesn't have to work."

"Oh, I don't know."

"You have to come."

Gran, she doesn't say anything. I'm not worried, though. Mama will drive me to the party. She always does. And Gran will come with us, and she and Mama will stay and have a good time.

Lordy, it is hard to pay attention in school today. Not only is Halloween tonight, but tomorrow and Friday there is no school so the teachers can go to their annual meeting down in Wyatt. Miss Casey is nice about our noise and fidgets, though, and when we come inside after recess she even surprises us with cookies and soda before we put on our costumes for the parade.

"Well, here is my Mickey Mouse costume," I say loudly as me and my classmates rummage around for our things. "Darryl, where is your devil stuff?"

"It's right here," says Darryl as he pulls the red hood out of a bag and holds it up.

I hear a small titter then and find HRH Vanessa looking my Mickey head over. "I guess you made that yourself," she says.

"I always make my costumes. Don't you?"

"No. My mother makes them for me," replies HRH grandly. She is putting on this ruffly dress and these lacy mitteny things and a bonnet of frills.

Well. Mama has never once made a costume for me. She is not really one for creative pursuits. That is my department. I bet HRH's mother has never taught her shorthand squiggles, though.

"What are you supposed to be?" I ask Vanessa.

"Why, I am Little Bo Peep. This costume won me an award in the Mechanicsville Halloween Festival Parade last year."

I could not care less about HRH's darn award. I just want to be plain sure that everyone in our class knows I am Mickey Mouse and Darryl is a devil.

The parade is fun. Mr. Walter himself hands out prizes at the end. I don't win a prize, but HRH, she wins for the most beautiful costume in our class. She gloats at me. But all I can think about is the Halloween surprise that me and Darryl and Clarice are planning.

The Coker Creek Elementary School Halloween party always begins at six-thirty on the nose. By then, it is full-on dark. On this Halloween, the air is as cold and the sky as clear and the stars as sparkly as a Christmas Eve. Mama drives Gran and me down the hill in our old car. We rattle and bump along and talk about when we might be able to have the heater fixed. The Mickey costume is in a pillowcase on the seat beside me, the paper head folded up neat-like with no hard creases.

"What time is church, Adele?" Gran asks Mama for the one millionth time since Mama has said we have to hurry through supper to get to the party.

"Not church," Mama reminds Gran. "The Halloween party at Belle Teal's school."

"With the haints and ghouls," I say helpfully.

"Where are your church gloves at, honey?" is Gran's reply.

I don't answer.

When we reach the school I fly out of our car ahead of Mama and Gran. "See you later!" I call. I have to find Darryl and Clarice. We agreed to meet in the hallway by the library.

I am the last to arrive.

"Hurry!" whispers Clarice loudly.

No one is around, but we are not taking chances.

First me and Clarice help Darryl put on the Mickey costume. Last thing, he pulls off his shoes, and tugs on those boots. Then he and Clarice help me with the devil costume, and I put on Darryl's sneakers, which we already know fit me because we had a trying-on.

Clarice, she is a hobo. The hobo and the devil and Mickey walk calm-like down the corridor to the all-purpose room. I do not know about Darryl, but my heart is pounding.

We stand at the entrance to the party. "Darryl," I whisper, "over there, that's my gran and my mama. Just in case they try to talk to you or something. Did your parents come?"

"Just my father. My mother had to work. She was afraid because Winnie and Terrence weren't allowed to come, but I said I really wanted to go to the party.

So my father drove me, but he's waiting outside in our car. In case there's any trouble."

I adjust the eyeholes of the devil head. "Okay," I say. "Let's go."

We have not taken more than four steps when a monster, a vampire, and a mummy surround us. It is Little Boss, Vernon, and Chas. Little Boss, he edges closer and closer to me until he is stepping hard on my toe. When I try to pull my foot away, he steps down even harder, but I refuse to let on that he is hurting me. I don't know if Darryl sees what is happening, but he says in our squeaky Mickey voice, "Hey, you guys! Let's go play some games."

I want to take just a moment to look around the room, which is all decorated with the orange and black decorations we have been making during art, and hung with streamers and fake cobwebs. A big orange moon is rising over the refreshments table with its plates and plates of cookies and cakes and Halloween candies and the big punch bowl. All of our teachers are in costumes, and a few of the parents are too.

The parents who have stayed for the party are grouped up at one end of the room, talking and laughing and eating. I see Mama and Gran with Mr. and Mrs. Baker. I look around for Big Boss and am relieved when I don't see him. If he thought that under the devil costume was one of the Negro kids, well . . . a shiver runs down my back and I shake it off. Then I remember the day Darryl walked to school by himself for the first time, and how he hurried along like a monster was after him. I shiver again.

I have to catch up with Clarice and Darryl. They are halfway across the room by now. I start to squeeze through the kids who are crowded around the game booths. It is easier than I thought it would be. Every one moves aside for me. I am pleased — until I feel the wet spray around my eyes as somebody spits at me. My stomach rolls over and I have to take in a breath. Then I raise my fist to clobber whoever did that, but it occurs to me that Darryl would never hit someone, and besides if I start a fight I will spoil our surprise.

So I wipe off my eyes with my sleeve and keep going.

Clarice and the boys are at the penny-pitch booth. Darryl, he is hanging back, letting the others go in front of him. As I catch up with them, I hear Little

Boss say to Darryl, "You go first, Belle Teal." He is being awfully nice to me, I think, but then, Halloween is his favorite holiday. Maybe he's trying to make up for all his meanness lately.

Mickey Mouse steps up and starts pitching pennies. He isn't very good. I watch him, wishing I could yell out, "Go, Darryl!" but of course I can't.

Just as Darryl loses completely, someone whomps into me from behind. I turn around and see a sixth-grader dressed as a bat. He's glaring at me. I hurry to Clarice's side for safety.

"Come on, Darryl, you take a turn," Clarice says to me.

And at that, Little Boss, Vernon, and Chas stalk off. They pull Mickey Mouse after them.

"Look at them," I whisper to Clarice.

"I know," she whispers back.

It's like the boys are trying to prove to Darryl that I am their friend. I have not been very nice to them this fall, I think. Darryl and Clarice and me have been our own little group for weeks now. But then I think of name-calling and spitting and shoving and I remember why I started to ignore Little Boss and them in the first place. This is a very complicated thing.

Me and Clarice follow after Mickey Mouse and the boys.

"Oh, Lord, there's Vanessa," says Clarice as we push through a group of kids at the apple-bobbing tub.

HRH is coming toward us with a cup of purple punch from the refreshments table. We are all set to walk right on past her, haughty-like, when suddenly she seems to trip and she falls forward and spills the entire cup of punch down my devil shirt.

"Oh, *my!*" she exclaims. "Look what I have done to your costume, boy."

I notice that she does not say she is sorry. I want to point this out, but know that Darryl would not do that. It is up to Clarice. She does a fine job.

"Vanessa Mathers, there was nothing there for you to trip over," she says at full volume. "You did that on purpose."

I am peering downward, trying to see what my front looks like. The stain is huge. I feel terrible until I remember that this is just one of Shari's hand-me-down costumes. I don't think Clarice will mind too much.

Still, now when the other kids look at me they point at the stain and laugh. I feel like I have wet my pants.

We catch up to Darryl and the boys. They are standing at the refreshments table. I see Darryl trying to fix himself a plate of food, but his Mickey gloves are making things difficult. Little Boss, he notices and says, "Here, Belle Teal. Let me help." He has not been so polite to me since the end-of-school party last June.

Little Boss piles a plate with cookies and candy. I see Chas and Vernon watching him. When Little Boss hands the plate to Mickey and says, "How's that?" they start to snicker. And a strange feeling creeps over me. I think maybe Little Boss has a crush on me. Which I have suspected before, but he has been so horrible this year that I have forgotten about it.

Darryl accepts the plate and the boys move on.

Is Little Boss ever going to be surprised when me and Darryl take off our costumes, I think.

Clarice and me wait on line for cups of punch. When I finally reach the head of the line and hold out my hand to take the cup from the punch-server, the kid behind me reaches out and grabs it first. And the kid behind her grabs the next cup.

I am thirsty, but I decide to step over toward Mama and Gran for a moment. I am hoping to draw a little comfort from them even though they don't know who I am.

"Adele," I hear Gran say to Mama, "what are all these haints doing at church?"

I leave quickly. I am separated from Clarice, and I feel nervous. For the rest of the party, I do not leave Clarice's side. Sometimes we hook up with the boys, sometimes we are on our own. It is almost nine o'clock, just before the party is to end, when we manage to whisk Darryl away from Little Boss and Chas and Vernon. Darryl is holding a ball and paddle, a prize Little Boss won for him at the ring toss.

"It's time to take off our costumes," I whisper to Darryl. "The party is almost over."

"I feel kind of bad," says Darryl. "Little Boss is being so nice to me."

"That's the point," I say. "Let's show him who he had so much fun with all night."

Clarice calls the boys over to us. The six of us are standing right in the middle of the whole party. "One, two, three," says Clarice.

And Darryl whips off the paper Mickey head while I pull off my devil hood.

Little Boss and Chas and Vernon stare at us. So

do a bunch of other kids. They are so quiet that for a moment it seems to me the whole party is quiet. That is not true, though. There is still a roar of noise around us.

But the boys' faces, they are not at all what I pictured every time I imagined this moment. Suddenly I see what I have done. My knees go weak and I grab onto Clarice's hand.

Thirteen

In the next second, Chas flicks forward like a snake's tongue and throws his whole plate of food on the floor. Then he lunges for Darryl with his hands in fists. Quick-like, me and Clarice jump in front of Darryl.

"Hey!" I say to Chas. "Don't you touch him."

Chas looks around and sees a teacher nearby, so he backs off.

Then Travis, this fourth-grader, he looks at Little Boss and laughs. "You!" he cries. "You gave your prize to the *nigger* boy!"

"He —" Vernon starts to say.

"You all spent the party with him!" Travis is hooting at Vernon and Chas and Little Boss, whose faces have turned bright red.

A small crowd of kids are collecting around us, but suddenly Little Boss, he isn't looking at me or Darryl or any of the kids. His eyes have lifted up and moved across the room. I look where he is looking and my own eyes fall on Big Boss. He is slouched by the doorway, leaning against the wall in a pair of dirty jeans, his jaw working on a wad of chewing tobacco. He is glaring at Little Boss.

How long has Big Boss been watching? I wonder.

Now Darryl and Chas and Vernon and Clarice, they all see Big Boss too. Behind me, Darryl starts to back away. Clarice's eyes get huge, and Chas elbows me roughly in my ribs and says, "Nice going, Belle Teal."

I have a huge fear of Big Boss, but I have to look at him one more time, like peeking under a Band Aid at a scrape. So I do. The expression on his face doesn't change, but very slowly he raises up his hand and crooks his finger at Little Boss. Little Boss walks across the room to him and they disappear into the hallway.

Chas and Vernon look at Clarice and Darryl and me with disgust. I do not know what to say to them, so it is a lucky thing when Gran scuttles up to me and says, "There you are . . . honey. Sunday school is over. Time to leave your friends and get on home."

I have never been to Sunday school in my life, but this is not the time to go into that. I grab Darryl by the wrist and say, "Come on. We'll walk you out to your car."

Clarice is running off to find her parents. "Come over tomorrow!" she calls to me.

"Okay," I say, and I am having trouble catching my breath, even though I have been standing still.

I try to calm down a little. Then I introduce Mama and Gran to Darryl and thank the Lord that Gran does not call me Lyman or say anything further about church.

"Darryl's father is parked outside," I say to Mama.

Mama does not know what happened at the party and I do not plan on telling her about it, but she did see Big Boss, so now she takes me by one hand and Darryl by the other, and says, "Let's walk on out together then."

Mama, she does not miss a trick.

I am shaking as we leave school, but Big Boss's truck is nowhere in sight.

"There's our car," says Darryl, pointing.

I peer inside it, trying to get a glimpse of Mr. Craig, but all I can see is someone very tall wearing a hat. As Darryl climbs into the car I give Mr. Craig a cautious wave, and he gives me a little wave back before he drives off. Soon me and Mama and Gran have driven safely up our hill.

The next day is Thursday, but it feels like Saturday, I think because of no school and the party the night before. I sleep late. But the moment I wake up I shoot out of bed. The very first thing I remember is Big Boss. The picture of him leaning against the wall and eyeing Little Boss comes into my mind and won't leave. I try thinking of fun things — making my costume and the parade and cookies and candy — but they all lead to the party and our Halloween trick.

What have I done to Little Boss?

I pull out my journal and write everything down. Then I get dressed and go into the kitchen. There's Gran singing "Waitin' for the Train to Come In" and looking over a collection of bottles and jars and packages that are spread across the table.

"What's all that?" I ask her.

"Why, I'm getting ready to make our fruitcakes," says Gran.

I can't help smiling. That is a very good sign.

I head on to Clarice's as soon as I have done my chores. I tromp down our hill in my too-tight boots and look at the trees, which are nearly bare. I use my thinking time to go over the results of the Halloween trick. All I wanted was for the boys to see that they could have fun with Darryl. But Big Boss showed up. And Little Boss . . . I suddenly remember that maybe he has a crush on me. Everything is a confusion.

I am in a state by the time I get to Clarice's, even though I am cheered by the bunch of dried corn on the Bakers' front door.

Clarice answers the bell when I ring, and she looks like she is in a state herself.

"Let's go to your room and talk," I say while I am still taking off my coat.

"We can't. Shari's in there with Patsy and Deanna, and Deanna is crying about a boyfriend."

The only place Clarice and me can get some privacy is in the Bakers' rumpus room, which is in the basement with their bomb shelter in case someone foreign drops a missile on us. Mama and Gran and I do not have a bomb shelter, but Clarice says we can always go to their house if a war starts.

We sit on the rumpus-room couch and drink Cokes and help ourselves to a dish of Halloween candy.

"I've got to talk to Little Boss," I say. "This is killing me."

"Call him, then," says Clarice, waving her hand toward the phone.

"I can't. They don't have a phone, remember?"

"Then let's go over there."

"And run into Big Boss? Are you kidding?"

"It's Thursday. He should be at work."

"With Big Boss, you never know. I'm not going over there."

We lean back in the couch and each eat a Tootsie Roll.

"Your grandmother thought you all were at church last night?" Clarice says after a moment.

"Yeah. And I'm not sure who she thought I was. Maybe Mama, when Mama was little. She was talking about Sunday school and church gloves. You know she made Mama and Lyman go to Sunday school and church every single Sunday while they were growing up. That's why Mama won't hold with church stuff now."

"But how could your grandmother look around the Halloween party and think she was in church?"

"I don't know. How could she look at me and call me Adele? Or *Lyman?*"

Clarice shrugs. We are stumped.

"Want to watch TV?" asks Clarice.

I shake my head. I don't want to go upstairs. I want us to be alone. But there isn't much to do down here. We try looking at one of Shari's fashion magazines, but it just isn't us. Hairdos and makeup and all.

"Do you think we'll ever care about this stuff?" Clarice wants to know. She is wrinkling her nose at a photo of a girl about Shari's age who's holding up a tube of lipstick.

"Maybe when we're older," I say. I don't want to rule out any possibilities. Then I heave an enormous sigh and add, "One thing, Clarice, do you think Little Boss might have a crush on me?"

Clarice drops the magazine. *"What?"*

"I don't know. Last night, when he thought Darryl was me, he got him a plate of food, and he won him that prize and all. And you know how he's always teasing me. Could be that he likes me."

I half expect Clarice to laugh, but she does not. Instead, all serious-like, she says, "I guess it could be. Lord, no wonder he was so embarrassed last night. It wasn't even just our trick. Or that Big Boss saw him get tricked."

"I know." Now I feel more miserable than ever. I decide there is nothing to do but wait until Monday and talk to him at school.

On Monday morning I am the first one off the bus. I fly down the steps and along the walk to the front door of Coker Creek. When I get to our classroom I look inside. Little Boss isn't there yet. I will wait for him by the door.

I wait until the last bell has rung and Miss Casey is about to take attendance. No Little Boss.

He shows up the next morning, though. I am posted by our door again. Clarice, Chas, and Vernon, they are all in the classroom.

"Little Boss!" I cry when I see him.

"Hey, Belle Teal," he answers. He does not sound too mad. Then I notice that he is holding his notebook and lunch and everything all in one arm, and keeping his other arm pulled against his chest.

"What's the matter?" I ask. "Did you hurt yourself?" I try to roll back the sleeve of his jacket for a better look.

Little Boss jumps a mile.

"Take off your coat," I command.

"No."

"Well, you're going to have to. Miss Casey won't let you wear it inside."

Little Boss shrugs out of his jacket. His left wrist is in a splint.

"What happened?" I say, suspicious-like.

"I fell down the stairs. That's why I didn't come to school yesterday."

"How did you fall?" I want to know.

"I just fell is all."

"Well . . . Little Boss, about the party. I'm sorry —"

But Little Boss walks ahead of me into the classroom. "Come on. We don't want to be late."

"But I really am sorry —"

"Don't mention it, Belle Teal."

I don't. I never mention it again. And when Chas and Vernon see Little Boss's splint, they don't mention it either.

Fourteen

I am not one for bragging, but I have to say that the fruitcakes me and Mama and Gran make every year are some of the best in the county. Now, I am aware of the unfortunate reputation of fruitcakes. They have a funny name, and people joke about there being just the one fruitcake that gets passed around from person to person year after year. Plus, as Mama says, some fruitcakes have a weight problem.

But our fruitcakes are really something special. They do *not* weigh a ton. And they are made from Gran's secret family recipe, which among other things, calls for marmalade and bourbon. Followed by a special aging process while the cakes sit in their tins in bourbon-soaked cheesecloth for several weeks, which is why we always bake our cakes on the day after Thanksgiving. If we want to give them as Christmas gifts, they'll have just enough time to age before we start handing out the tins.

Those tins, we collect them all year long. At Christmastime we save the ones that arrive at our house with cookies and candied nuts and things in them. And anytime we go for a long drive in the countryside we scour the shelves of junk shops and what Gran calls anteeky stores. We find little tins and big ones, tins shaped like squares and octagons and rectangles and ovals, and tins with all manner of pictures on them — funny-looking old-fashioned children with angel wings and enormous eyes, glorious Christmas trees lit with candles, country cottages by vegetable gardens that put ours to shame. My favorite tin, it was one I found last year, and it showed all these dogs sitting at a table playing cards. I asked Gran if we couldn't put our own fruitcake in it, just so's I could look at the dogs for another year.

One night in November, directly between Halloween and Thanksgiving, I finish my homework, and me and Gran and Mama decide to sit in the parlor by the fire together for a while. Mama, she has just taken some big tests and she has a night off from school.

"Got all A's," she tells us. "Never did that before in my life."

"Mama, that's wonderful!" I exclaim.

"Thank you, precious." Mama lets out a stream of smoke and Gran gives her the eye.

"Mama, where we going to have Thanksgiving this year?"

"Right here. I promised Cousin Tic and them that we'd have the dinner this time."

Goody. All our cousins from Penny County.

"Thanksgiving, then fruitcakes," I say. My mouth is watering at the thought of all that wonderful food. First our turkey and biscuits and gravy and sweet potato pie and Cousin March's sausage stuffing and Cousin Carrie's berry pies plus Gran's pecan pie. The next day, the fruitcakes with all their glorious ingredients.

"We better start a list," I say. I get up for a pencil and a piece of paper.

"A list of what?" asks Mama.

"Who we're going to make fruitcakes for."

I begin to write: the Bakers, Miss Casey, Bernette, Miss Wanda, a little one for Little Boss. "Mama, who you want on the list? Anyone new from school?"

Mama sighs, thinking. She stubs out a cigarette and lights up another.

"Merchant, put that pipe out," says Gran. "It's a filthy thing."

Now Merchant is Mama's daddy who left Gran about twenty years ago and then turned up dead in the Foggy River.

"It's a *cigarette,* and I just lit it," says Mama sharply. "I'm not going to put it out now." She is very tired, I can tell. I notice, though, that she doesn't correct Gran on her biggest mistake. Mama puffs away. Then she says more soft-like, "I don't know how I'm going to be able to help you all with the fruitcakes this year." She says this like a confession. "I'll have Thanksgiving day off, of course, and I might get one other day off, but Mr. Titus isn't sure. If I do get another day off, it better be the one before Thanksgiving so's I can help cook. But the fruitcakes . . ."

"Don't worry, Mama," I say. "Gran and I can take care of things. We can cook the meal and . . ." I trail off as Gran gets up and wanders out of the room. "And we can make the fruitcakes too."

I am not certain about this, though. Especially not when Gran comes back into the parlor wearing that flimsy nightie of hers, and nothing else. Outside, it's freezing. Inside, it's freezing too, unless you're in the kitchen or within five feet of the parlor fire. These days the grass crackles with frost every morning and the wind whips around the corners of our house. And Gran is wearing her short cotton nightie and bare feet.

"I believe I'll make myself a sandwich," she says.

We finished dinner no more than an hour ago.

I look at Mama. She looks at me. Then she shakes her head ever so slightly and picks up her cigarette again.

I am scared about Gran, but the next day Miss Casey takes my mind off of things. As soon as she has taken attendance and written down our lunch and milk orders and all, she says, "Girls and boys, it is time to talk about our school Christmas program."

I feel a great joy. To my mind the Christmas program is the highlight of the school year, maybe even of the whole entire year. Every class in Coker Creek Elementary takes part in it, and all the parents and grandparents and little brothers and sisters and even some aunts and uncles and neighbors go to it. Last year our class wrote Christmas poems and read them aloud. The year before, we sang two Christmas carols, and also a Christmas song that we wrote ourselves. The program starts off with the songs and poems and readings, and leads up to the very best part, which is the Christmas pageant itself. Each year, one class is chosen by a drawing (out of a felt hat in the teachers' room, I think) to put on the pageant. I have never yet been lucky enough to be in the class that gets chosen for the pageant, although I am always hopeful. After the pageant everybody, students and guests, traipses into the cafeteria, where a big old Christmas feast is held. We all bring something for it, and it is a sight for sore eyes — pies and cakes and cookies and hams and turkeys and casseroles and biscuits and oh, it's just tables and tables so full of food, it could take your breath away.

Our program, it is almost as good as Christmas day itself. Which is why a murmur of excitement runs through the room now.

Miss Casey is grinning a wide grin. She says, "And

I have a wonderful piece of news for you. Our class has been chosen to put on the pageant this year."

I can barely stop myself from jumping out of my seat and cheering.

"Yes, this is very good news," Miss Casey goes on, looking at our faces. "It's a great honor. I am sure we are all up to the job. I will assign the roles for the pageant this afternoon. Right after recess."

Then, since Darryl and HRH Vanessa don't know about our Christmas program, Miss Casey describes it to them. "After the pageant," she adds, "we have a wonderful party in the cafeteria. Everyone contributes something to it. This year I would like each of you to bring in something that you have made at home, preferably from a cherished family recipe. Take a moment to think about what you might like to bring in and then I will make a list on the board."

While we think, Miss Casey, she writes "CHRIST-MAS FEAST" across the blackboard, and then lists our names in two columns. When she has finished she turns to us. "Junie? I'll start with you."

"Well, my mama makes molasses cake," says Junie.

"That's just fine," Miss Casey replies. She writes "molasses cake" on the board next to Junie's name. Then she calls on Mae.

"Peach pie, with our own preserved peaches," says Mae proudly.

Miss Casey adds "peach pie" to the list.

As the list grows longer, my mouth begins to water.

"Vanessa?" Miss Casey is saying.

HRH stands up beside her chair and says all hoity-toity, "*I* will bring in my mama's fancy Noel lace cookies. They are French, I believe." Then she sits down again.

"Lace cookies" is added to the board.

"Darryl? How about you?" asks Miss Casey.

Darryl is looking shyer than ever, like he might be tongue-tied, but he manages to say, "Chocolate-chip cookies."

Finally it is my turn. "My gran and I will make our fruitcake," I say.

I hear a faint snicker from Vanessa's side of the room. Let her laugh, I think. I know for a fact that nobody has tasted anything like Gran's recipe. It has been in our family for decades. Plus, over the years Gran has perfected it. She has made so many changes on that dirty, sticky, flour-covered recipe card that the writing is hard to read. But every year Gran deciphers it. And every year the fruitcakes get a little better. They're expensive to make, but somehow we always manage to buy enough ingredients for our large quantity of cakes.

I ignore the snicker and announce, "I guarantee it will be the best fruitcake you will ever eat."

"I'm sure it will be," Miss Casey replies kindly.

During recess me and Clarice and Darryl are generally left alone. Which is a good thing because we do need to get our writing time in. We have a whole notebook full of *City Lights* episodes now. Today I am scribbling away as Darryl, he is telling me a good idea about a fire in a shoe store, when a shadow falls across the book. I look up. There is Vernon, standing in front of us with his hands in his pockets and a frown in his eyebrows.

"What?" I say, rude-like. I do not feel like being interrupted. Plus, I do not know whether to trust Vernon after the Halloween surprise.

"You," Vernon says, pointing at Darryl's chest like he is only a can of soup on a store shelf, "do not need to bother bringing in those cookies. No one is going to eat *your* food."

I leap to my feet but Vernon is not finished. "You're not going to be in the pageant either," he says. "There's not going to be any part for you. Colored people had nothing to do with the birth of Jesus Christ."

Very slowly Darryl gets to his feet. "I believe you're wrong about that," he replies.

But Vernon is already stalking off.

Fifteen

Vernon doesn't cause any more trouble, and me and Clarice and Darryl go back to Miss Casey's room after recess with a new episode of *City Lights* in our notebook.

We have barely sat down at our desks when Miss Casey, she says, "And now I will assign the parts for the pageant."

HRH's hand shoots up. "Oh, Miss Casey," she trills, "aren't we going to try out for the parts?"

"Well, there are no speaking roles," Miss Casey replies, "except for the narrator. So there is no reason to try out. I have given this some thought, and I have made my choices."

Miss Casey explains that with nineteen of us in the class she has included a lot of shepherds, some townspeople, and a barnful of animals, so's we can all have parts. She stands before us holding a piece of paper. "Listen carefully," she says. "I will call out your name, then I will call out the part you will play. If you have any questions, please hold them until I have finished reading the list."

Miss Casey leads off with the main characters, and the first one is the narrator. Guess what. Clarice gets that part. She is a very good reader and speaker, so that makes sense. The next role is Joseph, which goes to Stephen Haines. After that is Mary. I about faint when I hear Miss Casey say, "Mary: Belle Teal Harper."

Well.

You could hear a pin drop, I think that everyone, including me, assumed that the role of Mary would go to Vanessa. And frankly, I was hoping to be a rooster, because I have a collection of colorful feathers I can use on my costume. But no, Miss Casey, she clearly pronounced *my* name after she said "Mary."

So there is a tiny scuffle in the air of the classroom, but Miss Casey makes like she doesn't hear it and just continues on.

The Three Kings are next. Miss Casey, she says, "Walter Dunney" and "Ray Stomper" for the first two kings. Then she says, "King Gaspar: Darryl Craig."

Miss Casey pauses for a second or two after she says this, like she expects some sort of noise, even though she told us to hold our questions. Sure enough, a couple of kids cannot contain themselves. I look around and see a lot of open mouths and frowny foreheads. Then Vanessa cries, "Hey!" entirely forgetting that proper ladies always raise their hands. And Vernon, he calls out, "There wasn't any ni — any, um, colored people in the time of Jesus Christ, Miss Casey."

"Ma'am, he can't have that part," adds HRH.

"And why not?" replies Miss Casey, looking around at all of us.

"Because of what Vernon just said," Vanessa answers.

"Well, I am afraid Vernon is wrong." Miss Casey puts down her list and stands with her arms crossed.

"Okay, maybe there were colored people back then, but they were slaves," speaks up Mae.

Miss Casey remains calm. "Many people believe," she says patiently, "that one of the Three Kings was King Gaspar, a dark-skinned man from India or Africa." She looks around at us a moment longer, then says she won't entertain any more comments or questions, picks her list back up, and continues reading from it. I realize that Miss Casey still hasn't said HRH's name, which means Vanessa is going to get stuck with one of the itty parts. I am fascinated.

Miss Casey doesn't say Vanessa's name until she gets started with the shepherds. I can't help looking over at HRH to see her reaction. She slumps down in her chair. Cast as a shepherd, losing the part of Mary to me, and a colored boy given the role of a king. This is surely a bad day for Vanessa Amy Wynona Mathers.

I find out just how bad when school ends and Clarice and I climb onto our bus.

"Hi, Bernette," we say.

"Hello, girls."

I lean into Bernette and whisper, "I'm going to be Mary in the Christmas pageant!"

Bernette grins, showing the spaces where her teeth are missing, and says, "Good for you, honey!"

"Will you come to the program so's you can see me?"

"I wouldn't miss it."

"Thank you!"

Clarice and I head down the aisle. And the next thing I know, I am sprawling. I fall on my hands and knees, and my books go scattering, then my knees give way and I am lying on my stomach in the aisle of the bus with faces peering down at me from the seats above. I hear Clarice say angrily, "Vanessa, you tripped her on purpose," which I already know.

In a flash, I am on my feet. A hundred thoughts wheel around in my head, things I would like to say to Her Royal Highness. But I can also hear Gran saying, "Fight your battles with words, not fists, Belle Teal." What do I find myself doing instead? I lunge for Vanessa. I am about to grab onto a hunk of that blonde hair of hers when two strong hands separate us and HRH thuds down into her seat with a little cry.

"Bernette, what did you do that for?" I say. Bernette, she almost never interferes in our kid business. I thought she knew better. And I thought she was my friend. A true friend would let me fight this fight. I almost disinvite Bernette to the pageant, but then I turn my back on everybody and stomp down the aisle toward Clarice, who has gathered up my books for me. As I huff into our seat, I shout to HRH, "Vanessa, you're just mad because Miss Casey asked me to play Mary instead of you. Well, you are a big, spoiled baby. You can't have everything your way, you know."

Everyone is quiet after that. Even the boys don't say anything. Later, when Bernette has urged the old bus up our hill I stalk down the aisle, past HRH, who won't look at me, and to the top of the steps, where I hesitate.

"Still want me to come to the pageant?" Bernette asks like she is some kind of mind reader.

"I guess," I say.

Inside our chilly house I find Gran in the rocker by the fire. "Is you is or is you ain't ma' baby," she's singing. She looks like she might be lost in some world in her head, but when she sees me her face lights up. "Belle Teal, tell me all about school!" she cries, just like in the old days last year.

I'm so happy to find my regular gran that I don't say anything about what happened on the bus. "Miss Casey, she told us our class is going to put on the pageant in the Christmas program this year," I tell Gran.

"Well, my stars. The Christmas pageant. Isn't that wonderful."

"And something else," I say, trying to feel as excited as I felt before I got on the bus this afternoon.

"Miss Casey already assigned our parts in the pageant, and I am going to play . . . Mary." Even though I had wanted to be a rooster, the more I think about playing Mary, the Holy Mother of Our Lord Jesus, the more special I feel.

Gran places her hand over her heart. "Heaven above," she says. "Why, Belle Teal, that's wonderful."

I look at the expression on Gran's face and I think about the great thing I have been asked to do, the great thing Miss Casey thinks I can do. I decide not to let HRH spoil it for me. I hope Darryl is happy too, happy about playing a king, and then I think to say, "Gran, was one of the Three Kings a colored man?"

Gran stares into the fire. "Could be," she says. "There's all different opinions about such things."

I nod my head, and then Gran, she says, "We must think about your costume. I believe I have some blue fabric somewhere that would make a nice robe for you."

Gran doesn't call me Lyman once all night and I whistle her silly "Is you is or is you ain't" song while I wait for the bus the next morning. When it arrives I whisper, "Sorry about yesterday," to Bernette before I clomp down the aisle. Then HRH and me, we manage to ignore each other except for her faint little whistling about Beverly Hillbillies, which I guess is meant to convey that HRH thinks Miss Casey assigned a hillbilly girl to play the holy part of Mary. Well, so what. Vanessa can think what she thinks.

In school that day we are all abuzz with the program, and us and Miss Casey spend half an hour talking about the pageant. First there is the matter of our costumes.

"Each of you will be responsible for providing your own costume," says Miss Casey. "We can discuss what they should look like, and I will need to approve them when you bring them to school for rehearsals, but you will be making them yourselves at home.

"Now about Clarice's narration, we will work on it together in class. Clarice, you are welcome to try to memorize your lines, but if you prefer to read them, that is fine too.

"We will begin rehearsing in class after Thanksgiving, and later we'll hold dress rehearsals in the auditorium. Does anybody have any questions?"

Little Boss raises his hand. "I don't believe Darryl should be a king," he says.

I think he adds "with me" at the end of the sentence, but I am not sure because Miss Casey cuts him off and says in a sharp voice she hardly ever uses, "That is a comment, Ray, not a question, and I do not want to hear another word about this subject from any of you." Her eyes stray to HRH, and I remember the note HRH's father sent Miss Casey at the beginning of the year.

I look over at Darryl. He is sitting up straight, and I think I see pride in his eyes.

Sixteen

Thanksgiving Day turns out to be a pure delight this year. Mama does manage to get the day before off (although not the day after), so she and Gran and me just cook and cook on Wednesday. Even with all her forgetfulness Gran is still in charge, because she has always been in charge of the cooking. And because Mama really is a terrible cook. The funny thing is that Mama *likes* to cook. It's just that she hates to follow recipes.

From sunup to sundown we cook. Pies and vegetables and rolls and jellied things. Also, I spend two hours in the afternoon making place cards for the table. I want each card to be different and each one to be just right for whoever it's for. Like for Gran I carefully color some cooking items. And for Mama a typewriter. I have to make ten cards in all and it is quite a job. In the end I am proud of my work.

The next day — Thanksgiving! I wake up extra early and lie in my room in the dark and wonder about my friends and what they are doing at that exact moment. Clarice, she is probably still asleep. She is not an early bird like me. Darryl might be up already. He and his parents are going to drive for four hours to go to his granddaddy's house, where they will stay until Saturday.

After a while I listen for the sound of Gran getting up early, early, early to put the bird in the oven. "The bird" is what Mama calls the turkey. I don't hear anything at the usual starting-the-turkey hour, though, and when I get up to find out why, I run into Mama in the chilly kitchen.

"Where's Gran?" I ask.

"Still asleep, I think. I'll just start the bird myself."

This makes me nervous, but Mama does a fine job, so our day is off to a pretty good start.

*   *   *

Cousin Emery and Cousin Carrie and Cousin Samuel and Cousin March and Cousin Tic and the little ones, Stevie and Lacey, arrive at noon from Penny County. They have had a long drive and when they pile out of their cars they say they are starved.

Stevie and Lacey, we have to give them a little something to tide them over, but the others say they can wait. So first we all sit around in the kitchen and talk while dishes of food go in and out of the oven and on and off of the stove. An hour later we crowd around the two tables Mama and I pushed together in the parlor. Everyone admires my placecards.

The feast begins. Oh, there is so much food. Not as much as there will be after the Christmas program at school, but still quite a bit. I sample everything. The more we eat, the noisier we get. Cousin Tic, his voice grows louder and louder as he tells stories. Everyone laughs and gabs, and finally says what a wonderful job me and Mama and Gran did with the meal. Even Cousin Samuel agrees, and he being fourteen, which is just the worst age of all for a boy, that is some compliment.

Late in the day Cousin March says how they all

better be pushing off, they'll be driving home in the dark as it is. So we have to say good-bye. Lacey, she wraps her skinny arms around my knees and cries, "I don't want to go! Can't we stay one more hour?"

Cousin Carrie says, "Okay, one more hour," and then she pretends like an hour is a minute, and one minute later she says, "Okay, the hour's up. Time to go," and Lacey, she just says, "Okay," all happy-like.

When everyone has left and Mama and Gran and me have cleaned up the mess, we sit by the fire for a while. I imagine I am in two places at once — on the braided rug in our parlor with dreams of Christmas and pageants and fruitcakes in my head, and curled in the swing on our porch in the chilly air, watching the smoke from our fire wisp out of the chimney. Sitting there dreaming with Mama and Gran, that is one of the nicest moments of the autumn.

The next day, Gran is already in the kitchen when I stumble out of bed. I am relieved, remembering how she overslept the morning before.

In spite of the quantity of food I ate yesterday. I have my mind set on a big breakfast before we go to work. So I say to Gran, "I'll make breakfast while you get started, okay?" I think how nice it will be to surprise Mama with some of my pancakes to fortify her for the R U Sleep Inn.

"Okay," says Gran. "But . . . you stay over there." She points to the section of counter by the sink.

I look at the teeny area. "You mean I have to make the pancakes there? Can't I use the table?"

"Lord no."

"Why not?" The table is bare. There is nothing on it except Gran's elbows and the recipe card for the fruitcakes.

"Because . . ." Gran's voice trails off and she doesn't answer me.

I forget about the pancakes. "Gran," I say suspicious-like. "Where's all the ingredients for the fruitcakes?"

"Well, I don't know." Gran sounds vague.

"What do you mean, you don't know?" I run into the pantry, where Gran has been collecting things. Soon I am getting out marmalade and walnuts and slivered almonds and raisins and currants and citron and candied cherries and dried pineapple rings, flour and brown sugar, bourbon and spices. So many spices — nutmeg and cinnamon and cloves. Seven in all, including the salt. Then thirty-six eggs. *Thirty-six.* Since Gran always triples the recipe.

By the time our ingredients are lined up in front of us, Gran looks a little more like Gran. She helps me set out the baking tins and waxed paper and cheesecloth.

"Now may I make the pancakes?" I ask.

"Pancakes?" Gran replies. "Whatever for? We have to start the fruitcakes."

I study the tin with the card-playing dogs, which it is time to give up. I have decided that Clarice's family should get the tin this year. "I was going to make pancakes for Mama. You said I could, remember?"

"Of course I remember. Why are people always asking me if I remember?" Gran snaps.

This is not fair as I know I have been careful about not saying "Remember? Remember?" to Gran, like I sometimes hear Mama say to her. And who are these "people" Gran is talking about?

I am mad. "What people?" I demand.

"The . . . the ones who call on me and want to know things . . ."

"Morning, everybody!" says Mama cheerfully from the doorway. "My, you two are going to be busy today. I'll just grab some coffee and get on out of here."

Nobody wants my pancakes anyway.

When Mama leaves, Gran surveys the kitchen table. "Well, my land, it's fruitcake day, isn't it? We better get started. Where's the . . . the . . . that white thing."

"The recipe card? It's right over there."

"Goodness, Belle Teal. What would I do without you?" says Gran as I hand her the card.

That card, it is so ancient and dirty that I can't read it at all. And it is so worn, it feels like fabric. But Gran is not bothered by this. She squints at the card and looks at it from several different angles, then announces that we can get to work.

"First we cream the butter and the sugar," she says.

I stop myself from saying, "Are you sure?" because it seems to me that we always start with pouring the fruits and nuts into a bowl. I actually have my hand on the chopper to chop up the walnuts.

"All right," I say, and I reach for the butter.

We do things a little differently that day. We get it all done, just not in the usual order. Gran and me, we work and work, and outside, the day slips around us, weak morning sun and stronger noon sun and fading afternoon light. It is suppertime and full-on dark before Gran proclaims us finished. There are a couple of eggs left over plus half a jar of marmalade, and we didn't have quite enough raisins or candied cherries, so the fruit end of things is a little skimpy. Plus we went through much more bourbon than usual. Things haven't come out as even as in previous years. Still, Gran and I congratulate ourselves on our good work, and our house smells glorious, like Christmas.

I imagine my classmates sampling the fruitcake. I can see it all sliced up into polite little squares, laid out on napkins with poinsettias on them. Miss Casey herself tries a piece. "Oh, my," she says. "Why, this fruitcake gives fruitcake a good name. It is just delicious and it doesn't weigh a ton. You must give me the recipe, Belle Teal."

Next HRH Vanessa tries a piece. She doesn't say anything, but she licks her lips. Then she takes another piece. She can't help herself.

I decide that when that happens I will be very gracious-like and compliment her on her mother's French lace cookies.

Seventeen

Christmas is a fine holiday. There is nothing I don't like about it — the music and the decorations and the surprises and the presents and chopping down our Christmas tree. This year is even better, with our pageant and all. So I don't mind one bit when school starts up again after Thanksgiving vacation, because now there are only a few more weeks until Christmas, and in my mind they are the best weeks of the year.

I have been hard at work on my costume. I have taken four books about Christmas out of our school library, and I have been studying Mary's clothes. Mostly her outfit looks like a blue bathrobe with a hood. I kind of wish for a more interesting costume. It would have been fun to turn those feathers into a rooster outfit, or to glue cotton balls onto a leotard to make a sheep costume, or to make spangly wings for the angel Gabriel, or even to make one of those curvy sticks the shepherds carry. Still, it is going to take some doing to get Mary's robe just right, and now Gran, she doesn't seem to be a lot of help about it. I guess I am on my own.

One interesting thing is that in those Christmas books the pageant people all look different. I want to know more about the colored king, and when I go looking for him I see that in one book the Baby Jesus has black hair and in one book he has blonde hair, and those swaddling clothes never look the same. Each picture is different. Now the kings, in one book they are all definitely white. And a couple of books don't show pictures of them, but in the fourth there is a king with brown skin and black hair. I don't see his name anywhere, so I don't know anything more about King Gaspar, but before I return that book to Mrs. Harvey our librarian, I write down the title and author in case there is further trouble about Darryl and his part in the pageant. I want to be able to show the picture to Chas and Vernon and Little Boss.

One night after I have finished my homework, I pull out my costume. I have decided that I should make an attractive belt to go around the robe. One of the pictures I have seen shows a sort of rope around Mary's middle, but I think I could make something just a little fancier. I am sitting on the floor surrounded by a pile of yarn in all colors, and Gran has already asked me six times what am I doing. I don't know how to answer her any differently to get the point across.

Gran looks up from staring into the fire. "Why, Belle Teal," she says. "What's all that?"

This time I do not answer her directly. "I am so excited about our pageant," I say. "I still can't believe Miss Casey picked me to play Mary. This has been the best school year of my life. I have gotten almost straight A's, and me and Darryl got our Halloween book put right in the library for all the world to see, with an A plus on it. And now the pageant and the

Christmas program. Everyone is going to love our fruitcake, Gran."

"We better get started on that," says Gran, looking back into the fire.

One Monday morning, about two weeks before Christmas, I am waiting for the bus bright and early. I am hopping from foot to foot, but I hardly notice the cold. Today is the day of our first big rehearsal for the pageant. I have brought my costume with me so's I can show Miss Casey how it is coming along. I certainly am proud of the green and pink and orange yarn belt I braided.

The second that bus squeaks to a stop and the door *whooshes* open, I leap up the steps, call hello to Bernette, and start looking for Clarice. The bus seems quiet to me, but really all I can think about is the belt.

"Clarice! Look!" I cry as I spot her. I am pulling out the belt before I even sit down.

"Belle Teal," Clarice says, somber-like, and I think she doesn't like the belt.

"I know these might not be the right colors for Mary —" I start to say, suddenly concerned about what I have done, and that's when someone taps me on the shoulder from behind.

"What?" I say, turning around and stuffing the belt back in my costume bag.

Chas and Vernon are eyeing me darkly. "I guess you haven't heard," says Vernon.

"Heard what?" I reply. I glance at Clarice and I can tell that whatever it is, she already knows it too. I get a very bad feeling. Also, I am mad at the boys because they seem so eager to give me this news that I am probably not going to like.

"About Darryl. And Little Boss," says Vernon.

He is really dragging this out. Even Chas looks impatient, and finally he jumps in and says, "Me and Vernon went over to Little Boss's house yesterday and only Big Boss was there and he said Little Boss couldn't come outside because he's in the hospital."

"Because Darryl shot him," exclaims Vernon triumphantly.

I am stunned. Darryl shot Little Boss? The boys must have this backwards. They must mean that Little Boss shot Darryl. But no, that is not what they said. I feel my teeth begin to chatter. I think of our Halloween joke. Then I think of all that Little Boss has done to Darryl since school started. But still . . .

Everything about this seems wrong. And at first

the only thing I can think to say is, "If Little Boss is in the hospital, why wasn't Big Boss there with him?"

Chas and Vernon shrug. Then Chas says, "Don't you want to know what happened?"

I am not sure I do, but I say, "Okay."

"Well, Big Boss," Chas begins, "he came home from a job on Saturday afternoon" (I am thinking, more likely he came home from a bar) "and he found Little Boss bleeding in front of their house. Says he saw Darryl in the woods at the edge of their yard. And that Darryl had shot Little Boss with his hunting rifle. Little Boss is going to be all right, but he has to stay in the hospital until tomorrow."

Once again, this just sounds plain wrong. One thing, I know that Darryl doesn't have any hunting rifle. Two, if Darryl had shot Little Boss, why would he stick around and spy after?

"Darryl," I say slowly, "doesn't have a hunting rifle. He doesn't have any kind of gun."

"Then it must have been his father's," replies Chas.

"Darryl doesn't believe in killing animals," I go on.

"Just in killing white people," says Vernon.

I want to say, "Well, if that's the truth, then the

two of you will probably be next," but I clomp my mouth closed. I don't want to get Darryl into any more trouble. "I don't believe it," I say.

"It's what happened," says Vernon.

"There's no accounting for Darryl's kind," adds Chas.

I want to clobber both of them, but I look toward the front of the bus and notice Bernette glancing at us in the mirror. I swivel back and say in a loud whisper, "You mean to tell me that Darryl shot Little Boss, then hung around in the woods until Big Boss came home? Why would he want to be caught by Big Boss?"

Chas and Vernon shrug.

"Do you really believe Darryl went over to Little Boss's house and tried to kill him? Come on," I say.

"Well, he didn't go over there on purpose to murder him," says Vernon.

"Yeah, Darryl was out hunting and he was too close to the Stompers' house and he shot at a squirrel and hit Little Boss instead," says Chas. "I bet it made him real happy."

I still do not believe this. Not one word.

Bernette pulls the bus to a stop in front of Coker Creek Elementary, and what is the first thing I set my eyes on but Darryl and his mother and a tall man who must be his father all walking through the front doors of the school.

"Hey!" I cry. "Look! There's Darryl. You," I say to Chas and Vernon, "are crazy. You don't know what you're talking about. Darryl couldn't possibly have tried to kill Little Boss. If he had, he wouldn't be at school now, would he?"

"Darryl's been saying he didn't do it, says he was home the entire day," replies Chas.

Now that sounds more like the truth.

"Let's go," I say to Clarice. We are off the bus in a flash and running to our classroom. When we reach the doorway, there is Miss Casey talking quietly in the hall with Mr. and Mrs. Craig. We run by them and find Darryl inside sitting at his desk. I grab his hand and pull him to the back of the room.

"You hear?" he asks us.

"Chas and Vernon told us on the bus," I say.

"But we don't believe them," adds Clarice.

"What really happened?" I ask.

"Nothing," says Darryl, which is not what I expect him to say.

"What do you mean?" asks Clarice.

"I mean I wasn't anywhere near Little Boss's house on Saturday. I would never go over there. I was just at home that evening and a knock came at the door and my father answered it and a policeman was there and started asking me all these questions. Said Big Boss phoned them from the hospital — only he didn't say 'Big Boss,' he said 'Mr. Stomper' — to say he had come home to find his boy bleeding on the front porch and he had seen me in the woods with a hunting rifle and I must have shot Little Boss."

"What did your father say?" I ask.

"He told the policeman I was home all day, and that Reverend Watts — he's our preacher — was visiting. He stayed for hours. He knows I was at home too."

"So then everything is okay, right?" I say. "You're here in school. They didn't take you away or anything."

"Yeah, but it's our word against a white man's," says Darryl. "And you know who people are going to believe."

"They might believe Reverend Watts," says Clarice. "Everyone knows him."

All I say is, "Mmm." I am thinking of the look on

Big Boss's face when he showed up at the Halloween party and saw the trick me and Darryl had played on Little Boss.

Clarice is frowning. "Darryl," she says, "if you didn't do anything to Little Boss, then is he really in the hospital?"

"The policeman said he was," Darryl answers.

"So what happened? Why is he in the hospital?" I ask.

Darryl shrugs.

"Chas and Vernon said he'd be home tomorrow," Clarice reminds me.

I have this horrible heavy feeling in my head. Then my stomach starts to feel all watery, and I am afraid I might throw up. I am very worried about Little Boss, and very worried about Darryl.

Miss Casey steps back inside our classroom and calls us to order. I try to calm myself down. As I slide into my seat I notice how quiet the room is. Most of the kids are staring at Darryl. But Miss Casey, she claps her hands for attention so everyone shifts to her instead.

The morning passes okay. At lunchtime, Miss Casey hovers around Darryl and Clarice and me in case there's trouble, but she doesn't need to. Nobody treats us any different than usual. At recess, we even manage to write up a *City Lights* Christmas episode.

Later, when we have settled in at our desks again, Miss Casey announces that our first rehearsal is going to have to wait until the next day, as the third-graders need the auditorium this afternoon. I do not know if this is true or not. I think maybe Miss Casey wants to be sure there isn't going to be any trouble about Darryl.

"Bring your costumes to school tomorrow," Miss Casey tells us. "We will have a dress rehearsal."

At the end of the day, Mrs. Craig appears at the door to our room to walk Darryl home. Clarice and me, we walk close behind the Craigs on our way to the bus. In the hallway a bunch of kids turn and stare at Darryl. And then I hear a loud, papery "Ssssss," and I see HRH Vanessa hissing like a serpent at the Craigs, so I march up to her and stomp on her foot and don't even look back when she cries out.

Eighteen

Little Boss doesn't come back to school until Wednesday. On Tuesday, we have our very first dress rehearsal. We hold it after recess, and we get to use the auditorium and the stage. A few students are hanging around in the hallway outside, curious. But Miss Casey will only allow our class in the auditorium. We are as excited and noisy as a flock of geese, and Miss Casey doesn't want us any more riled up.

We have one problem with the pageant, though, which is that we are missing one of our kings.

I think Miss Casey is feeling sorry for HRH

Vanessa and her teeny tiny role, because she says to her, "Vanessa, just for today, would you like to be our third king?"

I think what a big spoily Vanessa is with even Miss Casey giving in to her whining sometimes, but HRH surprises me by answering, "No, ma'am." She pauses. "Thank you."

Miss Casey looks surprised too. "Are you sure?"

"Yes, ma'am. Thank you, but only boys should play the kings."

Hmm. I think what Vanessa is saying is, "Only white boys should play the kings."

"All right," says Miss Casey crisply. "Well, then, who would like to take Ray's part for today?"

A couple of hands go up, and Miss Casey chooses a different shepherd to be the king. She looks like she wants to choose Clarice, the only girl who raised her hand, but Clarice needs to practice her narration lines.

The rehearsal isn't quite a disaster, but if it had been the real thing, the audience would have been hooting and snickering at us for certain. Tinsley Ashburn's donkey costume looks more like a cat. Vanessa has chosen pink ballet slippers as her shepherd shoes, pointing out that shepherds weren't girls either (which I don't know if that is true or not), so who can say what shoes they would have worn? Stephen Haines's Joseph costume isn't bad, but Stephen won't stand any closer than three feet away from me, I think because I am a girl, so Miss Cascy decides there will always have to be something in between us onstage — the donkey or the manger or whatever — so's we won't look strange standing so far apart.

I am annoyed with Stephen. It is ridiculous for his fear of girl cooties to get in the way of our pageant, and on Wednesday morning as me and Clarice step off the bus in front of school, I say, "I am going to have a talk with Stephen today. If he thinks —"

I stop talking when I hear brakes screeching and see Big Boss's pickup parked sloppily in back of our bus, its engine idling. Big Boss slithers out of the driver's side, then hustles around to the passenger door and opens it for Little Boss. Little Boss, he climbs out very, very careful-like, carrying a pair of crutches. He sticks the crutches under his arms and hops along the walk to the front door, Big Boss at his side, holding Little Boss's lunch and notebook, a cigarette dangling from between his lips.

Clarice and me stand back and watch in awe. We have never seen Big Boss treat Little Boss so nice.

Big Boss walks Little Boss all the way to our classroom. He takes a long look in the room before he leaves, and I am afraid he is going to do something, although I don't know what, but he just swaggers off.

As soon as he's out of sight, I run to Little Boss, who is trying to settle himself and the crutches at his desk. His lunch falls on the floor and I pick it up for him. "Here you go," I say.

"Thanks." Little Boss stuffs the bag in his desk.

"So what happened?" I ask. "Is your leg broken?"

Little Boss looks at the bandage on his foot. "No," he mumbles.

"Is the bullet —"

I am still speaking when Clarice, she pulls me away and steers me to my desk. "I don't think he wants to talk about it," she says.

Darryl appears in the doorway a few minutes later. He has walked to school by himself today. When he sees Little Boss, he draws in his breath. I know he's expecting shouting or mean words, something hurtful, but Little Boss does not look at him. He will not look at anybody.

All day long, Little Boss is tied up inside himself.

He hardly talks. At recess, he stays inside with Miss Casey, his foot propped on a chair. Me and Darryl and Clarice try to write a New Year's Eve show for *City Lights,* but I am having trouble concentrating. I cannot stop remembering Big Boss as he walked Little Boss into school this morning. The more I think about it, the more I think Big Boss only looked pretend-kind.

We have another rehearsal in the auditorium that afternoon, and Little Boss, he has to sit down the whole time. Miss Casey allows as how she might have to rethink Little Boss's role in the pageant. But maybe his foot will be okay by Christmas.

Little Boss is still all quiet and drawn in like he was this morning. It is while Miss Casey is walking around talking individually to kids about their costumes that I see Little Boss sitting forward, holding his head in his hands. I break away from Clarice and Darryl and guide Little Boss to the back row of the auditorium.

"Little Boss?" I say. "What's the matter?"

Little Boss is wiping his eyes furiously with his sleeve.

I don't want him to feel too embarrassed, so I say, "Maybe you got something in your eye."

Little Boss shakes his head. "No."

"Does your foot hurt?"

He shakes his head again.

"Is —"

"Belle Teal, Darryl never hurt me," Little Boss says suddenly.

"I know." And then I have to say what I say next. "It was your father, wasn't it? He did this to you."

Little Boss jumps. "No! That isn't it. I did it. It was my fault."

"*What*? You shot yourself?" This cannot be.

"Not on purpose."

"But *you* did it?"

"Yes. It was an accident."

"Well, why did you say Darryl did it?"

"I *didn't*." Little Boss's voice is trembling, and his eyes are about to spill over again. "I told my father what happened. I told him the whole truth. I told him I was fooling around with his gun, which I am not allowed to do. And it went off and shot my foot."

"So why —"

"And he — he just wouldn't stand for that," Little Boss goes on, and the tears are running down his cheeks and any minute now someone is going to notice us. "I'm sitting there bleeding, and my father is mad at me for being stupid enough to shoot myself.

'People are going to think this is my fault,' he's saying. 'They'll think I don't know how to take care of my own kid. I told you and told you not to play with that thing.' He's calling me stupid and saying what a stupid thing I did to him. To *him*, Belle Teal. I'm bleeding, and he's yelling about how I did a stupid thing to him.

"Next thing I know he has this look in his eye and he makes up that story about Darryl and the squirrel and the hunting rifle."

I am seeing so much more than what Little Boss is saying. In my mind the whole autumn is falling into place. I am wishing for my journal, which is neglected, lying somewhere under my bed because I have been writing essays for Miss Casey instead of thoughts for my journal. But I know that tonight I will find it and write all this out — how Big Boss's hatred of Darryl just grew and grew; grew bigger the more his words and shouts were ignored; swelled when he saw Little Boss fooled by Darryl at the Halloween party; and probably nearly burst when he found out Miss Casey had made Little Boss and Darryl kings together in the pageant. Then Little Boss goes and shoots himself, and suddenly Big Boss sees a way to get Darryl in trouble.

I shiver. I would not want to be Big Boss's son.

"Little Boss," I say, "we have to tell Miss Casey the truth."

Little Boss looks absolutely terrified. "No!" he says. "I mean, not yet."

"But we *have* to tell her. Darryl's in trouble for something he didn't do. In trouble with the *police*."

"I know, I know, but —" Little Boss pauses, licks his lips — "just . . . just give me until tomorrow, Belle Teal, okay? I swear I'll tell tomorrow. But first I have to figure a few things out. Don't say anything to anybody until then."

I glance around to see what Miss Casey's doing, and what do I find but she is watching us. Watching Little Boss and me. She gives us a long look before she turns back to the angel Gabriel's silvery wings.

When school ends that day, every single person in our class sees Big Boss's pickup parked out front, and Big Boss leaning against the hood with a cheekful of chewing tobacco, waiting for Little Boss.

I look around our room — at Little Boss, at Darryl, at Clarice, at Miss Casey, all of them troubled.

"Darryl," Miss Casey says gentle-like as we are

putting our coats on, "I believe I'll drive you home today."

"I'm coming with you," Clarice announces.

"You'll miss your bus," Miss Casey replies.

Clarice doesn't care.

Little Boss shuffles toward the door on his crutches, and I think he looks as lost as Gran sometimes does.

"I'll walk you to your father," I tell him, since I know Darryl is in good hands.

And so me and Little Boss set out down the hall. I carry Little Boss's notebook for him, like Big Boss did this morning. When we reach the doorway, I draw in a slow breath and step outside. Big Boss catches sight of us right away. A smile creeps across his face when he realizes I am helping Little Boss. We make our way along the front walk, and I can't help but remember the first day of school this fall when the walk was lined with those shouting parents.

The closer me and Little Boss get to Big Boss, the harder my heart beats until I think it might explode right out of my chest. Finally I can't take it any longer. We are twenty yards away from the pickup when I say to Little Boss, "Do you think you can manage this?" and I hand him his notebook.

"Yeah," replies Little Boss. "Thanks."

"I'll see you tomorrow," I say.

"Okay. Bye, Belle Teal."

"Bye."

I watch Little Boss continue down the walk, watch Big Boss watch him. And I see Big Boss's mean eyes suddenly narrow as he looks at something behind me.

I turn around.

Now Darryl is starting down the walk. Miss Casey is next to him, her arm across his shoulders. Clarice is on his other side, and she loops her arm through his.

I stand there and look from right to left — from Darryl and Miss Casey and Clarice, to Big Boss and Little Boss. Big Boss, at first he can't take his eyes off Darryl. But then all of a sudden he says something low under his breath, and straightens up and hustles into the truck, slamming the door shut behind him, leaving Little Boss to struggle in on his own.

I am not surprised to hear Big Boss gun the motor as the truck roars away.

Nineteen

I do not know it then, but that is the last time I will ever see Little Boss.

After school that day I sit with my secret for as long as I can stand it, which is until after dinner. By then I am bursting, and decide it will be okay to talk with Mama or Gran. But Mama is off studying for her secretarial exams, and I do not know how late she'll come home. And Gran, well, she goes into her room to get ready for bed and comes out a few minutes later in another entire outfit.

"Gran, you're not going to sleep in that dress, are you?" I say to her.

And Gran, she looks so confused that I feel something break inside me.

It is not the night to talk to Gran.

So I find my journal under my bed and turn to writing in it again. I scribble down all my thoughts about Little Boss and Big Boss and Darryl and this fall. I am so thankful that tomorrow the truth will be told and everyone will know who did what, and that Darryl was just a kid sitting at home visiting with Reverend Watts.

The funny thing, though, is that I keep waiting to get the glorious feeling about all this truth, but it doesn't happen. I fall asleep with a small, empty ache in my chest.

Mama is still asleep when I wake up the next morning. She has left me a note saying she didn't come home until after midnight last night, and that she is going to take today off from the R U Sleep Inn in order to study some more. I am glad about all the studying, but that ache in my chest is growing, and I really want to talk to Mama. Or to some adult. Maybe I can talk to Miss Casey after Little Boss does.

On the school bus that morning, Clarice just chatters and chatters about Christmas. I try to listen, but finally I have to tell her that I have a little headache, and then Clarice quiets down, but she is hurt.

I feel bad, but I have to focus in on Little Boss. He does not come to school, though. Right away I am worried. Oh boy. Big Boss and his temper. He would be some mad if Little Boss said he wanted to tell the truth about Saturday. Then I think, what if Little Boss ended up going straight to the police all by himself and now Big Boss is in jail? After all, Big Boss lied to the police.

My mind is a whirl.

If Big Boss is in jail, where is Little Boss?

I try to concentrate on other things. It is a busy day. We have a spelling quiz and we have to work on Christmas compositions and that afternoon we have another rehearsal.

At the end of the day I ask Miss Casey if she knows where Little Boss is, and she says no, and I see something worried in her eyes.

That night I can't stop thinking about Little Boss. I have a very bad feeling. I wait and wait for Mama to come home, my eyes following Gran as she wanders around the kitchen in her summer nightie, humming "Juke Box Saturday Night," and later saying that my, this is the coldest summer she can ever recall.

To my relief, Mama comes home just after nine

o'clock. She has not even sat down yet when I say, "Mama, I have to talk to you. It's important." Then I surprise us both by bursting into tears.

Mama, she puts her arms around me and holds on tight until I calm down enough to talk. Then I say, "I know the truth about Little Boss and Darryl," and I tell her what Little Boss told me.

"But he didn't come to school today," I add, "and I don't know why. I should never have told him he had to tell Miss Casey the truth." A new thought occurs to me. "Maybe he ran away!"

"Precious, whatever has happened, it isn't your fault." Mama searches through her pocketbook for a cigarette, but gives up before she finds one. She sits us down on the couch, leans back, and puts her feet up on a table, which Gran never used to allow us to do.

"Nothing you did was wrong," she says. "You had to give Little Boss a chance to deal with this in his own way. Someone does have to tell the truth, though. But it does not have to be you. Or Little Boss. I will talk to Miss Casey tomorrow, okay?"

I nod. "When?"

"On my lunch break. I'll drive over to school."

"Okay."

*   *   *

On Friday morning, I get on the bus trying to feel hopeful. Just because Little Boss missed school yesterday doesn't mean he won't be there today. I settle next to Clarice, and am staring out the window when Chas and Vernon invade my thoughts.

"Guess what," says Chas.

I am tired of his games. "Just tell me," I say.

"We went over to Little Boss's yesterday and no one was there."

"So?"

"He means no one lives there anymore," says Vernon.

"What?" I exclaim, and Clarice looks up from the book she is reading.

"It's all empty, the house," says Chas. "Their stuff is gone."

"They moved on," adds Vernon.

I think of a million questions, but I can't ask them because I am still the only one of us who knows Little Boss's story.

That morning I look at our classroom clock at least one million times. Mama's lunch break at the R U Sleep Inn begins at noon sharp. I figure Mama can be at school by 12:10 if she leaves work immediately.

Chas and Vernon haven't wasted any time spreading the news about Little Boss around school, so Miss

Casey heard it the second she stepped into our class-room, and right away she disappeared down the hall, probably to talk to Mr. Walter. But she won't know the full story until Mama arrives.

Which is at 12:13. I am sitting in the cafeteria eating lunch with Clarice and Darryl, but mostly I am keeping an eye on the hallway. At exactly 12:13, I see Mama enter Coker Creek Elementary, carrying her red pocketbook, which is her good one, and wearing her fancy coat over the Adele uniform. She heads for the school office.

I don't know exactly what happens after that, and I don't care too much, just as long as the grown-ups take care of everything.

What I do know is that at the end of the day, Miss Casey, looking pale and very, very tired, tells us what we have already heard, which is that Little Boss won't be a part of our class anymore. She says that we will miss him, and adds that we will have to find ourselves a new king for the pageant. Which is how Trey Bee-ber, the shepherd, becomes a permanent king.

It is not until sometime the following week, though, that Miss Casey moves Little Boss's desk out of our room. One day it is there, the next day it is not.

Twenty

When I wake up on Saturday, the day after Mama comes to school, I feel limp and exhausted, like I've had the flu. Just for right now I can't think about white people hating colored people and fathers who shouldn't be fathers and boys with bruises. I do think about one thing, though — that I did right when I told Little Boss to tell Miss Casey the truth.

Mama reminds me about that time and time again over the weekend. And she takes a whole afternoon off from her studying so's she and I, just the two of us, can have lunch at the counter at Sherman's, and then look for a Christmas present for Gran.

On Monday, Darryl gives me glorious news. He says the police went to his house on Saturday and told them they got word that Big Boss had made up the story about Darryl. They are white policemen and they don't apologize to the Craigs, but they let them know Darryl is off the hook.

And so at school we get on with things. The news about Darryl spreads quickly. We keep up with our rehearsals, and Trey does a fine job as our new king. Also, we get our costumes in order. Except for Vanessa, who insists on those pink ballet slippers as her shepherd shoes.

On the Friday before Christmas, Mama comes home with an early gift for us.

"I have received my secretarial certificate," she says. She holds it aloft for Gran and me to see. "And now I am looking for a job in Mechanicsville. I believe I will find one by the new year. First thing, once I get a job, I am going to pay back the school account."

I look up from where I am sitting on the floor in front of the fireplace. "Are you really going to get a job in an office, Mama?" I imagine Mama going to work wearing nylons and skirts, and blouses with ties at the neck. She will sit behind a desk with a typewriter and a plant on it, working for a boss who calls her Mrs. Harper, only he pronounces it like Mizz Harper, but that's okay. Mama will be such a good secretary that her boss, he will constantly say, "Mizz Harper, what did I ever do without you?" Mama is beginning to seem like a character in *City Lights*.

"That's what I'm looking for," Mama replies.

"And you'll only have to work at one job and you'll be home for dinner every night?"

"I hope so, precious."

I feel so joyful that I leap to my feet and run into the kitchen, where I turn on the radio full blast and twirl the dial around until I find Christmas carols, and then me and Gran and Mama sing along with them for the rest of the evening.

Christmas keeps us all so busy that before I know it, it's the last day of school before vacation, the day of the pageant and the program. I wake up that morning the way I have waked up for I don't know how many mornings now, which is thinking about Little Boss. I wonder where he and Big Boss are, how Little Boss's foot is healing, if Little Boss is already enrolled in a new school somewhere. Or maybe Little Boss and his daddy are on the run from the police.

I feel my heart start to pound, so I play the trick I have taught myself. I pretend my mind is a fairy tale, and I tell those thoughts that now I have to banish them, and poof, away they go. Except that they always seem to sneak back the next morning.

I am enjoying a nice little rest in my warm bed when I catch sight of my Mary costume draped over the back of a chair. And suddenly I am full awake. I dress in a hurry and rush into the kitchen. I decide I had better eat a good big breakfast because I won't be able to eat again until after the pageant and it will not do for Mary's stomach to grumble onstage. I am eating scrambled eggs and biscuits when I hear the grinding of gears and know that Bernette is coaxing the bus up our hill.

"Uh-oh," I say. The Mary costume is waiting in a bag by the door, but the fruitcakes, they are still in the pantry.

"What's wrong?" asks Gran.

"The bus is here, and I haven't packed up the fruitcakes yet. The ones for the school program."

"Don't worry, honey," says Gran. "Your mama and I will bring them with us this afternoon."

Mama has taken another day off work so's she can go to the program. I consider waking her up to tell her about the fruitcakes, because I don't trust Gran an inch. But I don't want to embarrass Gran, so a few minutes later I am running to the bus, the bag with my costume in one hand, the fingers of my other hand crossed tightly.

"Where's the fruitcakes?" is the first thing Clarice says as I slide into our seat.

I make a face. "I was late. I didn't have time to get them. Gran said she and Mama will bring them this afternoon."

Clarice raises her eyebrows at me. I think she is going to say something about how maybe it isn't wise to trust Gran with such a task. Instead, she says, "I wonder what Vanessa is up to."

I glance at the front of the bus. HRH Vanessa is sitting there with her legs crossed, very prissy. I realize she didn't oink or smirk or hum the song about the Clampetts as I passed by. She barely even looked at me, and now she is just staring at the back of Bernette's head.

That morning Miss Casey tries to get us to concentrate on our studies, but of course we can't. At last she decides that one final pageant rehearsal might count as some sort of social studies lesson. So we gather up our costumes and head for the auditorium. A few minutes later, our costumes on, I find myself standing next to Vanessa, who has been unusually quiet all morning. I am about to edge on over to Clarice, when I decide it wouldn't kill me to be nice to Vanessa for once. After all, this is not a very good day for her, what with her wanting to be Mary and the part going to me and all, and now she has to play a shepherd and everyone has been teasing her about the ballet slippers.

So I say, trying my hardest to forget about all our fights, "Your mother hemmed your costume perfect, just like you said she would."

Vanessa nods and turns away.

How rude.

I tell myself HRH doesn't matter, and I am not going to let her ruin this day for me. I turn my attention to hoping Gran remembers to bring the fruitcakes to school.

Around eleven o'clock it begins to snow. I love snow, but now I think, please, please don't let the program be canceled. Not when I am going to play Mary. But an hour later our guests begin to arrive. And Miss Casey, sounding as excited as I feel, announces that it is time to go back to the auditorium. "Remember your costumes!" she calls as we line up at the door.

Miss Casey leads us single file through the hall and into the auditorium. All us Coker Creek students are going to sit in the front rows whenever we are not on-stage. Clarice and Darryl and me make sure to grab three seats together. We turn around and look behind us at the parents and grandparents and little brothers and sisters and other special guests.

"My parents are here," says Darryl, craning his neck around. "They're sitting with Winnie and Terrence's parents and Mr. Walter."

My excitement is growing, especially when I spot Mama and Gran, and Mama holds a bag up high to let me know she has the fruitcakes. I smile. I am *so* happy Mama is here. She told Mr. Titus she just had to have another day off, that she wouldn't miss this for the world.

That auditorium is noisier than a hundred school buses full of kids. Everyone is talking and laughing. The adults are calling, "Merry Christmas!" to each other.

The kids are talking about Santa and presents and choir practice.

Just when I think I can't wait another second or I will explode, Mrs. Portman, our music teacher, steps onto the stage and welcomes our guests to the Christmas program. The auditorium is dim, the snow falling outside the tall windows, and the room is hushed except for little rustlings and scrapings and here and there a cough. An enormous wreath with a red ribbon is hanging at the back of the auditorium, and a decorated tree is standing at one end of the stage. It is like all of a sudden I am wrapped in Christmas.

Our program goes grade by grade, starting with the littlest kids and ending with the oldest ones, but skipping our class since the pageant is last. Each class files onto the stage, sings carols or puts on a skit or reads poetry, then returns to their seats in the auditorium to watch the rest of the program. It is fun, but I am getting fidgety, waiting and waiting.

At last Miss Casey signals to me and my classmates, and says quietly, "It's time to begin."

She leads us out of the auditorium and backstage while Miss Carner's class finishes reciting "The Night

Before Christmas." As we put on our costumes, I hear applause, and then Mrs. Portman announces something called the P. S. de resistance, which I am not sure what she's talking about, but the next thing I know, the auditorium is absolutely silent, so it must be time to begin. Me and Stephen arrange ourselves with our donkey, Tinsley, between us so's Stephen doesn't have to stand too close to me.

Clarice steps in front of the curtain. She begins to tell the story of the Nativity. Our pageant has begun.

As far as I can tell, nothing goes wrong. Nobody seems to notice HRH's ballet slippers. I don't think anyone can tell that my husband, Joseph, thinks I have girl cooties. At just the right moment I lift Clarice's old Tiny Tina doll, who is supposed to be our Baby Jesus, out of the manger and I do not drop her. Most important, nothing happens when the Three Kings walk onto the stage. I do not hear one boo or hiss. But also, I do not see Little Boss under one of the gold crowns. Little Boss would have liked to walk onto the stage wearing a crown, even if Big Boss did not come to see him.

When the pageant ends, it is time for Miss Casey to run down the list of who played who. After she reads each name I hear a big round of applause, with especially loud clapping from the family of the person whose name has just been read. Like for Clarice — clap, clap, clap, clap from the audience with CLAP, CLAP, CLAP, CLAP from her parents. For me — clap, clap, clap, clap from the audience with CLAP, CLAP, CLAP, CLAP from Mama and Gran. But for Darryl all I hear is a little clapping, which is probably his parents and Winnie's and Terrence's, a few teachers, and Mama and Gran and Mr. and Mrs. Baker. Otherwise silence. No booing, but no big roar of clapping. It reminds me of Darryl's first day in school, when he introduced himself and then no one wanted to ask him any questions.

After the last name has been read and Mrs. Portman has thanked everyone for coming and our guests are making their way into the cafeteria, me and my classmates charge backstage and change out of our costumes. We are shouting and laughing and excited about the feast and Christmas and the snow. That's when I spot HRH silently slipping her costume back into its bag. She's off by herself. All morning I have been waiting for her to say something to me — something mean, anything at all — but she has been so quiet. She reminds me of Little Boss on the day he told me the truth about Darryl. I walk right by her carrying my Mary costume, and still she says nothing.

Me and Clarice, we hurry into the cafeteria and first thing, I search the crowd for Mama and Gran. There they are. Then I scan the tables for our fruit-cakes. And there they are.

The next few minutes are taken up with showing our own personal guests where to get plates and forks and so on. I give Gran and Mama a tour of the food. The fudge and biscuits and pies and chicken. "And those," I say at last, "are the French lace cookies Vanessa's mother made."

I look around for Vanessa and see her standing with a little boy and a man in a fancy suit, her brother and her daddy, I guess.

"Come on. Let's get plates," I say.

It is at this point that I notice a small commotion over at the dessert table. This one lady, her hand to her mouth, which is all pursed-like, is pointing to something and saying, "Why, there's enough liquor in those to . . . well, a person could become inebriated."

"What's 'inebriated'?" I ask Mama.

She doesn't answer.

Another lady says, "Don't let any of the children near them."

I push my way to the table. Whatever they are talking about, I want one.

"Clarice, Clarice, what is it?" I whisper loudly.

Clarice, who has been watching the commotion at close range, says, "Belle Teal, it's your fruitcakes. Do you put liquor in them?"

I feel the ground wobble beneath my feet. "They soak in bourbon," I reply.

"How much?"

I am about to say, "Not that much," when I remember the day after Thanksgiving and how the ingredients didn't come out even like usual. I feel my face begin to flush.

The fruitcakes are whisked off the table and carried out of the cafeteria.

Twenty-One

Belle Teal?" I hear Mama's voice behind me.

I whirl around to face her and Gran, ready to give Gran what for.

And then I notice Gran's vacant face. Where is she? Not here with us.

I start to say something anyway when Gran looks at Mama. "You better go count that church money now, Lyman. The people are going to need it soon."

Mama leans over and says quietly to me, "You just go and enjoy yourself, Belle Teal. I'll take care of Gran."

"But the fruitcakes —"

"*And* the fruitcakes. Don't worry. Go on. This is your special day."

Not anymore, I think. I shoot arrows at Gran with my eyes because I hear an awful lot of laughter from the direction of the dessert table. Then I turn and stalk away.

And bump directly into Vanessa.

We look at each other for a few seconds, then HRH, she lowers her eyes.

"Well, go ahead. Say something," I tell her.

"About what?"

"The *fruit*cakes."

Vanessa, her eyes are filling with tears, and I am not sure why. Here is the perfect opportunity for her to humiliate me. She's been snickering about the fruitcakes since the first moment I mentioned them.

"Well, I guess I better go have one of your mother's French lace cookies," I say. "I'm sure they're *much* better than our fruitcakes. Did you try a piece yet? Oh, that's right. You can't. Me and my gran made a mistake with the recipe and they took our fruitcakes away. So you win, Vanessa. Everything about you is better than me. That's what you've been saying all along, isn't it?

I'm a mess and dirt poor and I hang out with a colored boy and me and Gran and Mama are just white trash. You're rich and pretty and have perfect clothes and go to Europe and your mother bakes French lace cookies. Why don't you introduce me to your mother? That way you can make yourself feel even more special."

I have hardly noticed that now HRH is full-out crying.

I am not sure what to do, or what, exactly, I said that made her cry. "Where *is* your mama?" I ask.

Vanessa shakes her head.

"Didn't she come today?"

"No."

"Why not? Is she sick or something?"

Vanessa shakes her head again. "No. She's dead. I don't have a mother."

I am stunned. I stand there with my mouth hanging open. At first all I can think to say is, "Well, who made the French lace cookies, then?"

"My father and I. We made them last night. They're not as good as my mother's." Vanessa dabs her eyes with a Kleenex.

"Well . . . well . . . I'm sorry." I don't know what else to say. Questions are flying through my head, but it doesn't seem polite to ask them. I want to know why Vanessa talks about her mother like she's alive, and I want to know about that Halloween costume of hers, along with a number of other things.

Vanessa's tears won't stop falling, and I look around helplessly. Thank the good Lord that Miss Casey and Mr. Mathers appear then. Mr. Mathers puts his arm around Vanessa and leads her off. I look at Miss Casey. "I don't understand," I say.

Miss Casey, somehow she knows what's going on. "Vanessa's mother died this summer, Belle Teal," she explains. "And Vanessa is having a difficult time."

Mrs. Portman taps Miss Casey on the shoulder then and says she needs to speak to her. I am left standing in a corner of the cafeteria, by a chair with a crumpled napkin on it.

I hear Miss Casey's words again.

"Vanessa's mother died this summer."

That means her mother died just before Vanessa started coming to Coker Creek Elementary. The Matherses probably left Mechanicsville to get away from their old house and its memories. I have heard of such things, and I sort of understand, even though I think I would want the memories. No wonder Vanessa is so upset. She knew that today everybody would find out she has lied about her beautiful, perfect mother; that there is no mother at all. Vanessa kept this a secret all fall. But she must have realized that on the day of the Christmas program, when absolutely every parent shows up at school, her secret would come out.

I have to sit down for a moment.

I am slumped in one of the plastic cafeteria chairs when Clarice and Darryl find me. I know they think I am sitting alone because of the fruitcakes, and they aren't sure what to say to me.

So finally I say, "Everyone's been eating your cookies, Darryl. They're almost gone."

"Yeah," says Clarice. "Nobody thought to ask which food on the table is yours."

"And nobody did anything when Miss Casey read out your name at the end of the pageant," I point out.

Darryl considers this. "Yeah," he says. Then he adds, "I think my parents are having a good time. They're over there talking to your mom, Belle Teal. And to your parents, Clarice."

"To Mama? Where's Gran?" I exclaim.

"Talking to Winnie's parents. It's okay."

I look around the cafeteria and spot Gran holding

a cup of punch and talking to Winnie's parents. For a moment I wish for my old predictable Gran, the one who would realize she's in a school cafeteria and not in church; the one who would know how to follow a recipe so's not to make inebriating fruitcake. Instead, I see my new Gran, the one who's wearing two sweaters and has no true idea where she is. But she looks happy enough, so maybe she's all right.

My mind returns to its new piece of information.

"You know why Vanessa's mother isn't here?" I say.

"Why?" ask Clarice and Darryl together.

"Because she's dead."

Clarice and Darryl, they look as stunned as I felt. I tell them what happened.

"Huh," says Darryl. "I guess you never know about people."

I realize that this is true. There's a lot we don't know about what goes on underneath people's skins. Or inside their brains. Vanessa. Gran. Little Boss. Big Boss.

Outside, the snow starts to fall harder, and some of the parents round up their kids and say the going-home things: time to put on your boots, find your book. Where is your sister, your costume? Remember to say good-bye to Miss Greene. Run and get our baking tin."

Mama comes looking for me then. "We'll never get our car up the hill if we don't leave now," she says. "You better say your good-byes."

"Where are the fruitcakes?" I ask her.

"Packed up."

"Are they really ruined?"

"Well, they are pretty strong, precious, but I don't think they're all that bad. Get your costume and your coat now."

Mama goes off to find Gran, and I look at Darryl and Clarice. "I guess I'll see you after Christmas," I say. "Seems like a long time from now."

"When school starts up we can work on *City Lights* again," says Darryl, and he grins at me.

We all say, "Merry Christmas!" and I tell Miss Casey good-bye until next year, and soon I am walking out of school with Mama and Gran, into the snow and the gray light of winter, the fruitcake tins in a bag carried by Mama.

I wait for a wave of awful feelings to wash over me. Disgrace over the fruitcakes. Shame for the things I said to Vanessa. Fear for Gran, for Little Boss, for

Darryl. I remember Darryl on that first day of school, remember the look on his face when he shook Miss Casey's hand and told her good morning. Then I remember the look on Big Boss's face as he slouched in the doorway at the Halloween party, and on Little Boss's face when he told me the truth about Darryl and the hunting rifle. I remember Little Boss's bruises, think how I actually believed he was clumsy enough to fall off his porch more than once. The awful feelings do wash over me then, just like they do first thing most mornings now.

My stomach jumps like it has been kicked. I try my fairy tale banishing trick, but it doesn't work. So finally I tell myself that if I can't eliminate the negative, at least I can accentuate the positive. I think of the first time Darryl gave me his smile, and of being an honorary Baker over at Clarice's; of Miss Casey, and of Mama with a secretarial job.

I slip one hand into Mama's and the other into Gran's and realize something: Gran's strength long ago flowed into Mama and me. We can take care of each other. And Mama and I will be able to take care of Gran. For the moment, I concentrate on feeling only the strength of this family of women, my family.